THEM

ASHLEE NIX

Content Warnings

- Death

- Murder

- Dubious Consent

- SA

Playlist

- Just Pretend by Bad Omens

- The Loneliest by Maneskin

- Fix You by Coldplay

- Scared by Joywave

- I'm Not Okay by Flora Cash

- Are You Really Okay? by Sleep Token

- The Night We Met by Lord Huron

- The Reason by Hoobastank

- Used To Love You by Gwen Stefani

- Dangerous by Sleep Token

- For Your Love by Maneskin

- All I Wanted by Paramore

- Chokehold by Sleep Token

- Missing Piece by Vance Joy

- All I Want by Kodaline

Love is love.

It is not louder when approved, Not less

when questioned.

It does not require translation or permission.

Chapter 1: Malsumis

NO! NO! NO! MY OLIVE! WHAT HAVE I DONE!
OLIVE! NO! NOT MY OLIVE!

Everything comes flooding through me. My memories. My power. I come down from the rush of everything and regain control. I cradle her in my arms. I pull her close, pressing my forehead to hers, my tears falling into her hair, and let out a roar of anguish so loud I can hear windows in the house shattering. I look down at her too pale skin. I have just killed the only person I have ever been in love with, the only one ever unconditionally to love me. This cannot be how our story ends. It will not be how our story ends.

I am a god. There are things I can do to save her. Letting go is not an option. Others who can help me. Yes, that is it. It is all coming back to me. I lie her on the carpet and unsheathe the knife that is at my hip. I make one cut above her heart and one on my wrist. I place my cut over hers and let my lifeblood flow into her. I watch as her cut heals, confirming that the exchange is working.

Now, I wait. I lie beside her and wrap my arm around her. Watching. Waiting.

After what seems like ages, my Olive takes a breath, and it is the most beautiful sound I have ever heard. I pull her close, and then I notice the bandage on her arm. I carefully unwrap it from her, and tears prick my eyes again. She had my feather drawing tattooed on her arm. It all hits me. She was going to surprise me with this and free me tonight. This is what she was planning. What she wrote in her journal was a momentary doubt because I am a god of chaos and destruction. I raise my tunic and see that her drawing of the broken arrows and circles is now permanently on my skin. She created a seal. One that no one would ever know what it was. They could not use it against me.

"My Olive, wake up. Please wake up. I cannot lose you. I love you. Please wake up. *Please.*" I pull her close to my body and whisper into her ear. She does not wake, though. Something is wrong. She breathes. She lives, yet she will not wake.

"I know you are listening. Take my soul, my strength, my future. Just help me bring her back," I beg to the other gods that I know can hear me. They remain silent.

"Please," I whisper, my voice hoarse from screaming earlier, "Please someone…anyone. I know I am not worthy, but Olive is. Let her live. Please." Still no answer.

The sky groans with thunder, and the earth trembles beneath us. I barely notice over my grief. I clutch her tighter, eyes shut, lost in despair. I feel the shift in the air, the warmth cutting through the winter's cold. I hear a crunch of footsteps through the broken glass behind me. I do not move. I cannot. Not until I hear his low, familiar voice cut through the silence.

"Hello, Malsumis," Set's deep, accented voice has me turning to see him for the first time in 270 years.

Chapter 2: Malsumis

"Set, please help me save her," I beg my oldest friend as he crouches down beside me.

"She lives Malsumis."

"She lives, but she does not wake. Please help me. I cannot lose her." I continue to beg.

"I heard your pleas. I am glad I answered and not another, or you would be bargaining your power right now, Malsumis. You must be careful."

"I will give up what I must to save her."

"Come with me to my home, and we may find help there." Set suggests.

I pick up Olive and hold her close as we dematerialize to travel to Set's sanctuary in his pantheon's lands. We arrive at his palace, and I follow him to his private wing. He begins to lead me to his room.

"Set, I am not putting my girl in your bed," I growl.

"Mal, it is the safest room in the whole realm."

"Fine."

I grit through my teeth.

We enter his room, which is decorated in the deepest greens and blacks, Olive's favorite colors. A fresh wave of misery runs through me as I lie her on the bed.

"I need to go see Thoth. He will know how to complete her healing," Set says. "You are welcome to stay here with her or wander about the palace as you wish, old friend."

"I will stay here with Olive," I say as I sit on the bed and take her hand in mine.

"I shall return as soon as I get answers, Mal." With that, he was gone.

I wasted no time in lying beside Olive and holding her close to me. Maybe I can reach her in our dream state and wake her that way. I close my eyes and breathe in her scent and drift off. I do not reach my Olive in our dreams. Instead, I relive that painful moment of no control. I feel her pulse beneath my hand, the break of her bone. I jolt awake, sitting straight up in the bed. I look over, and she is in the same position I left her in. I move to the edge of the bed, put my head in my hands, and weep.

Set returns sometime later in the night with news from Thoth. He does not look exactly pleased with what he is about to tell me.

"The good news is she can be saved. The bad news is the options and bargains that it may take to do so."

"I will do whatever I need to, Set."

"I never thought I would see the day that Malsumis would be so concerned with a human."

"She is no normal human. I love her. She is my mate, Set."

"I also never thought that I would hear those words from your mouth. I know many females who will be upset at this news," Set says, trying to lighten the mood.

"Set back to how to save my girl, please."

"Yes, well, is there any way that you could contact your brother or father?" He says, looking a bit nervous. My family and I have a…complicated history. Mostly, my brother is the golden child who does no wrong, and I am the outcast who does no right.

"Is this the only way?" I love Olive enough to do whatever it takes to save her.

"It would be the only way to keep her fully in your pantheon. Otherwise, she would be under yours, and ours, and the consequences of this are unknown."

"I shall speak with my father. Although I feel like we both know the answer I will receive," I respond.

"I will watch over your Olive while you are gone. No harm will come to her, I assure you, Mal."

"I am entrusting you with the most precious thing that I have ever had, Set."

"I understand," he replies.

With that, I go to Olive's side and kiss her forehead and whisper in her ear, "I shall return to you soon, my Olive. I will save you. I love you with all that I am." I back away from my love and go to see my family.

Chapter 3: Malsumis

I arrive outside my father's home, and it looks the same as it did when I last saw it over 1,000 years ago. It is not a palace like

Set's and his pantheon, but a humble home of logs built around the Tree of Life. Beside it, a crystal clear flowing sacred river that carries souls, dreams, and wisdom. Here, my father watches over the realm, but he does not rule from a throne as others do. He believes in balance and harmony. Everything here is peaceful and calm, everything I want to be for Olive but never have been before.

I know my father will not help me, and therefore, my brother will not help either. One reason is that they have never understood me, my hatred of humans, or my need for chaos. Another is that I disrupted the balance by saving Olive. I will not let this stop me, for Olive, I will face them and beg for help. I knock on my father's door.

"Enter Malsumis," his deep booming voice calls out. Of course, he knows I am here.

"Hello Father."

I walk to him in the center of the room, where he stands stoic and proud in front of the trunk of the tree. I have no doubt caught him in the middle of a ritual.

"Where have you been? We searched for you for many years, and there was no trace of you," he says, sounding concerned.

"I was trapped in the mortal realm by a summoning spell."

"You are here now, I am glad you freed yourself," all concern leaving his voice.

"I did not. I met a human female; she freed me. She is my mate Father, and she needs to be healed from an accident I caused. I am here to beg for your help to save her."

"I never thought that you would ever befriend a human, much less take a human mate. I am proud of you, my son. However, I cannot help your human. It will disrupt the balance of things."

"I have already brought her back, but she will not wake. Please, Father, help me. I know I am not worthy, but she is," I beg, dropping to my knees in front of him.

"Yes, I heard your plea earlier, but I must not intervene in this, my son," he says plainly.

"You heard me and did not answer? Did my brother hear as well?"

"Yes, he did as well, but he understands that he must not intervene either."

"I beg you to reconsider, father. I love her and cannot lose her. I will not survive it."

"My answer remains the same, Malsumis. The balance of life must not be tampered with. I am disappointed that you have done as much as you have."

"Father, please. I will do anything to save her. Please help me." I beg as tears stream down my face.

"My answer is no Malsumis," he says firmly.

"There is nothing left for me here then…Goodbye, Father."

"Malsumis…", I do not hear anymore because I am gone before he can finish.

Chapter 4: Malsumis

I arrive back outside Set's chambers after the disaster of a visit with my father. I wanted to travel back directly to Olive's side, but Set's wards prevent anyone but him from being able to enter any other way than the door, and even then, he must invite you in. I stand at the door and gather myself. What am I going to do now? It would have been so much easier for Olive if my father had helped. I understand not helping me, but Olive is innocent. A familiar voice draws me from my thoughts.

"Malsumis, I heard you were back, but I did not quite believe it," Eris says sweetly.

"Eris, I do not have time for niceties."

"Oh, straight to the fun stuff, hmm. I have missed you, too, Malsumis," she purrs, running a finger down my arm. I pull away from her. No one but Olive will ever touch me again.

"No, Eris," I growl as I knock on Set's door.

"Someone is grumpy. Come find me when you want to *relax*, Mal." She teases with a smirk.

Set opens the door, surprised to see Eris with me. I roll my eyes, and he gets the hint that it is an unwanted visit by the goddess. Set lets me in, and I head straight for my Olive's side. I hear a gasp from the hall right before the door slams. Eris saw her.

Shit.

"I'm sorry, Mal, I did not close the door fast enough," Set apologizes.

"She would have found out anyway," I assure him.

"I am assuming you have no good news from your family?"

"My father refuses to help, and you know my brother will stand with him. What other options do we have now?"

"I will speak with Father. He is informed of your situation and knows you have been found. He considers you part of the family, especially since you helped me protect him against attack during the uprising. I have no doubt he will help. Thoth says it is possible to wake her, and we will not rest until we do, Mal."

"Thank you. Shall I go with you, or can I stay with my Olive while you go to Ra?"

"You stay with her. I will come to you when I have news. I have food for you on the table in the adjoining dining room. No one is allowed in there either, so do not worry about being bothered," Set explains to me before leaving to visit his father.

"Truly, thank you."

Once Set is gone, I crawl into bed beside Olive and lie beside her, watching her breathe, trying to will her to open her eyes. I brush a strand of hair from her face, letting my fingers trace the curve of her cheek.

"Please, wake up, Love. I cannot survive without you. " I will not survive without you," I feel my voice cracking as I speak. "Olive, you have to open your eyes. Please, baby, come back to me."

I close my eyes and allow my power to flow through me to Olive. My magic flares in my veins, radiant and violent, but Olive remains silent and unmoving.

"Olive, you are stronger than this," I growl, my voice edged in desperation, "Do not leave me now." Nothing.

I clench my jaw as I choke back a sob, fury and heartbreak warring in my chest. Around me, the world seems to be holding its breath, waiting for me to lose control. I sit up and wrap my arms around Olive and pull her into my lap, as if my embrace could call her soul back from where it has gone.

"I will find a way to save you," I whisper into her ear, "Even if I have to tear the stars from the sky one by one. I will not lose you, Olive."

"That will not be necessary, Malsumis." Ra's booming voice shakes me from my despair.

"Hello, Ra, thank you for meeting with me." I greet him as I lie Olive back on the bed and cover her with the sheet. I bow to him; typically, I would not, but I need his favor today.

"See that Set, Malsumis knows how to greet me. You could learn a thing or two." Set rolls his eyes from behind his father, which I would usually laugh at, but I am in no mood today.

"Ra, this is Olive. She found me and freed me from being trapped in the human realm."

"Set filled me in on that much. Tell me, Malsumis, how did she die?" he asks. I drop my head immediately and try to formulate the words without sobbing.

"I…killed her. When my powers and memories surged back to me, I lost control momentarily, but that was all it took." I explained, keeping my head hung low in shame. Ra takes a deep, thoughtful breath.

"You have healed her in the sense that her body is whole. Her soul is far gone. Not unreachable, but you must retrieve it from the underworld. When you brought her here, her soul followed. You must go speak with Anubis," Ra explains.

"I will do what I need to do to have Olive back."

"I will take you to Anubis, and Set will watch over your human." Ra commands.

"I will not allow anything to happen to Olive while you are gone, Mal," Set tells me as I bend down to kiss my Olive before I leave.

"Let's go get your girl," Ra says as he claps me on the back and we disappear from the room.

We arrive in the Chamber of the Scales, the divine courtroom between life and death, where the hearts of the dead are weighed against Ma'at's feather of truth and balance. The room is dimly lit, with a blue black glow, and the air is thick with incense that smells of frankincense. Everything is quiet except the whispers and low cries of the dead and lost souls. At the center of the room are the scales that hum with power. Beside them stands Anubis, cloaked in black; all that can be seen are his seemingly glowing gold eyes. Beside him sits Ammit the Devourer, part crocodile, lion, and hippo. She sits awaiting the next unworthy heart she can devour, erasing that soul from existence.

"Father. Malsumis," Anubis greets us.

"Malsumis is looking for someone. " I will leave him to explain," Ra turns to me. "Malsumis, this is your journey. I have led you as far as I can; you must find your way now."

"Thank you for assisting me, Ra," I say with a slight bow, and he is gone.

"I am looking for a human. Her name is Olive, she has hair practically as light as snow and bright blue eyes…" I start turning to Anubis before he interrupts.

"I know whom you speak of."

"Where is she?"

"Not here," is all he replies. Panic stabs me in the chest.

"Where. Is. My. Olive?" I say through clenched teeth.

"I sent her on; she did not belong here."

"Anubis, where did you send my Olive?" I demand even as my knees threaten to buckle.

Chapter 5: Olive

Darkness. Vast consuming darkness. That is all there is here. It is not cold. It is not warm. It just is. The air is heavy and thick, and the silence is louder than any scream. I remember Malsumis. Then, I was being pulled here, like being unspooled from my body to wherever here is.

Shadows drift around me, not quite human figures, yet not formless either. These are others who came before me, who never found their way out. I try to panic, but I can't. I just am. I feel nothing. No pain. No sadness. Nothing.

Suddenly, there is a dim glow in the distance. It is faint. It seems unreachable. I am being pulled toward it, though. Whether it is hope or a warning, I don't know, but I want to find out.

I walk toward the light, purely on instinct at first. I feel the shadows try to pull me back with each step. Every step becomes more willing as I try to get away from the darkness. The light is small and distant, but there. It is difficult to peel away the shadows as I walk, but my resolve is stubborn, even as they try to remind me of the pain I have endured at the hands of my love. Some whisper. Some plead. I am steadfast, though.

The closer I get to the light, the more it begins to pulse. The closer I get, the more I remember the life that was taken from me.

I remember HIS touch, HIS voice, HIS hand around my neck. Suddenly, my heart feels heavy, and I hear it begin to beat.

I wake up. I take breath, shallow and ragged. The darkness is replaced with a blue-black glow, illuminated by torchlight along the walls. The air is heavily scented with incense. I am lying on a cold, smooth stone slab. I look to my left and see a wall carved with hieroglyphs. Where the hell am I? I look to my right and am staring directly at Anubis, the Egyptian god of the underworld.

Anubis stands before me, tall and still. His black jackal face mask peeks out from his black cloak. His gold eyes watch me without judgment. His eyes meet mine, not cruel yet not kind, but deeply knowing. His presence is heavy in front of me, but not in a threatening way. I glance behind him and see the great scales of Ma'at. I know where I am. How did I end up in the underworld of the Egyptian afterlife?

Anubis offers me his hand, and I take it without thinking, sitting up, then standing up beside him. We walk to the scales, and my heart manifests into his hand. I feel an emptiness but no pain in my chest. He says nothing as he places my heart on the scale opposite Ma'at's feather. What seems like an eternity passes. The feather doesn't rise, and my heart doesn't fall. They are balanced. I let out the breath I was holding. Anubis looks at me and finally speaks.

"You carry both shadow and light, but you are not yet meant to cross, Olive Ambrose. You do not belong here with me," he says in a deep, resonant voice that echoes through the hall.

"What do you mean? What am I doing here?"

"You were brought here to save your life by the one who took it. He seeks to bring your soul back as we speak. So you wish to return?"

"I wish to return to my realm, to my life."

"It is impossible to return to things as they once were, Olive. You are forever changed. If you return to your body, you will be new, immortal. While you can return to your realm, the humans cannot know what you are. You will never age as you once did. You will never have the life you once did."

I look at Anubis. Sadness for what I have lost seeps into my now returned heart. I'm angry that my choices have been taken from me and my life has been forever changed by someone who was supposed to love me.

"I am made whole here. Can I still visit my old home?"

"Yes, but as I said, you will be as you are now, and humans must not know what you are."

"What if I choose to stay as I am?"

"You will wander the darkness until it is your time to find your way out again."

"So, no choice really," I comment, and his eyes flash something almost sympathetic, "I choose to be made whole again."

"Very well, Olive. I wish you well." That is all he says before there is a bright flash of light.

Before I open my eyes, I can smell the perfumed fragrance of lotus and myrrh filling the air, warm and welcoming. Music hums faintly from distant harps and flutes. I open my eyes and blink. The cold stillness of Anubis's chamber is gone. Gone are the scales. Gone is the judgment and shadow. Here, I lie on a bed of embroidered linens and am clothed in delicate fabrics decorated with jewels and hieroglyphs. My chest still aches with the pain of the events that have transpired, and my heart is still heavy with them.

Someone is coming down the hall. I can hear their light footsteps and the sound of their jewelry. The door opens, and in walks one of the most beautiful women I have ever seen. She is radiant and serene. Her eyes hold joy, wisdom, and compassion as she looks at me. She smiles as she approaches me, sitting in the bed. I recognize her symbols. This is Hathor.

"You walked through the darkness, child. The gods have turned their eyes on you. HE is searching for you as we speak."

"Who?"

"Why, your mate, my dear. Malsumis."

"HE is not my mate! HE killed me!"

"An accident, dear one."

"An accident is tripping, dropping something. Not breaking someone you supposedly love's neck!"

"I understand, Olive. Just know he was not himself and would have never harmed you if he were in control."

"Noted," I say sarcastically.

"I like your...how do you say...moxy," Hathor giggles.

"Why did Anubis send me here to you? Why not just return me to my body?"

"I have a much more…delicate approach to the afterlife than my brother. I will be the one to return you to your body. I will give you this goblet, and you will drink from it. After that, you will sleep and wake up in your renewed body. Do you have any questions, child?"

"Can you keep my whereabouts from Malsumis? I do not want to see him."

"I am afraid I cannot. He is family here and is in Ra's favor…I will tell him to keep his distance if you would like me to, but seeing as how you are his mate, that probably will not work."

"I am not his mate! I am not his anything anymore!" I exclaim.

"Oh dear, you most definitely are his mate. I never thought I would see the day when he settled down, and he did well. You are stunning."

I would preen from such a compliment from a literal goddess under any other circumstance. But *MATE*. She keeps saying it, and I am really getting tired of this word. This cannot be happening.

"If you don't have any other questions, it is time to drink and be reborn as one of us. Your body is in Set's private quarters. No one can access them except Set, so you will be safe there until you recuperate."

"Should I be concerned for my safety outside of his rooms?"

"Malsumis had several…female companions, and one in particular may not be happy that he found his mate and that you are a human. He and Set will keep you safe, though, do not worry."

"Humph. I trusted Malsumis to keep me safe once, and here I am. Dead."

"Dear child, I promise you that was beyond his control. I know that feeling and wish it upon no one," Hathor says, eyes rimmed with sadness and regret.

"I'm ready," I say as I take the goblet and drink. It tastes of the sweetest wine. My sorrow eases, and there is laughter on my tongue. I feel warm, as if bathed in sunlight, and I begin to glow. Then I drift off to a dreamless sleep.

When I wake, I am in a massive bed with the softest, deepest, darkest green sheets that shimmer, turning almost black when moved. The bed is draped in heavy, black velvet curtains that hang off thick, twisted tree trunks supporting the canopy. The room is dark except for the torchlights on the walls and the candles placed around it. I look down from the bed, and the floor is stained ebony, with a beautiful hunter green plush rug with swirling black patterns spread out across it. There is a fireplace carved from stone on the opposite wall, and flames crackle behind the wrought iron grate. Bookshelves line the other side of the room, filled with old bound books and texts. That is where I find Set, the Egyptian God of Chaos and Destruction. He is sitting in a chair reading, seemingly oblivious to me sitting in his bed. I study him as he reads. He looks nothing like how I thought he might while studying Ancient Egyptian Gods in school. His face is commanding but not harsh; he has long, flowing raven black hair and a tall, muscular body with smooth tawny skin, which I see a lot of because he is barely wearing any clothes. He looks up from his book, sensing me staring.

"Hello, Olive, welcome home."

Chapter 6: Malsumis

"WHERE IS MY MATE?" I bellow at Anubis. True to his demeanor, he does not react.

"I sent her to Hathor. She has a gentler touch when it comes to these things," he calmly replies.

"What things, Anubis?" I snarl.

"Returning souls, turning humans to gods. Although there have been very few who have survived the transition. Your Olive seemed strong."

"I must go to Hathor's palace, now."

"You should hurry. Olive has long since passed through my chamber."

I do not say goodbye as I vanish from his cold, dark chamber.
I am met with bright light and surrounded by gold when I get to Hathor's. I hear the strumming of harps and the playing of flutes throughout the halls as I search each room for Olive.

"Ah Malsumis, I wondered when you would come," Hathor's light voice sounded from behind me, "Would you like to tell me why it is you are tearing through my palace like a crazed beast?"

"Hathor, you know why I am here. Where is Olive?"

"Hmm, Olive?"

"Hathor, I know she is here. Please, I am begging you to reunite me with her," I plead.

"She was here but is no more."

"Where is she now?"

"She does not want to be found *by you*. I am sorry. Know that she is well."

"I know she has not left this realm; she cannot until after her coronation into the pantheon. I will tear every palace, every chamber, and anyone in my way down to find her. Hathor, where is my Olive?" I threaten, becoming angry.

"I am gentle now, but do not forget who you speak to, Malsumis," she says with an edge to her voice.

"I am sorry. I did not mean to forget my place. I need to find Olive and be with her."

"She is quite hurt and angry, Malsumis. Do not expect a happy reunion. I have bought her as much time as I can, as I promised her. She is safe with Set."

She asked that I be kept from her? All of this was an accident; I was not in control. I must explain this to her. My girl is safe. She is whole, and that is all that I care about. I leave Hathor and go straight to Set's chamber. When I get to his door, Eris is waiting.

"Do you not have any business in your pantheon to attend Eris?" I ask.

"You certainly are one to speak, Mal. Anyway, I saw your pet. Is that why you are ignoring me?"

"She is my mate, and you will stay away from her, Eris."

"*Mate*? That human trash?"

"Watch how you speak about my girl," I snap, pushing her into the wall.

"Mmm, you remember how rough I like things," she purrs. I turn from her to knock on the door for Set, ignoring her. As soon as he opens the door, I slip in and slam it in Eris's face.

"You know she will keep trying to get back with you," Set says as I walk in.

"It will never happen," I reply as I head to the bed. I reach the bed, and Olive is gone. I whirl around and meet Set's gaze.

"Do not get angry, Mal."

"Where is she Set?" I say through clenched teeth.

"Listen, Mal, she is…hesitant about seeing you right now. Give her some time. Do not rush her."

"You act as if you know her, Set. She is MINE!"

"Whoa, I know. I have only spoken with her for the time she has been awake, and she has been…adamant that she does not want to see you."

"Please, I just want to see that she is whole once again and safe," I plead.

"She is one of us now and is safe. I cannot promise whole. There are pieces of her heart missing now," he says quietly. I understand what he is saying, and I know that those missing pieces are because of me.

He leads me to another bed chamber adjoining his, where Olive is. It is decorated much like his, except there are many more books in here. This is Olive's dream room, I am sure. In the corner, reading sits my Olive. She is radiant. Her snowy locks lie in waves past her shoulder. Her smooth skin has an ethereal glow, and she is dressed in a deep black linen dress with a deep V neckline and a fitted bodice. I let out a breath of relief.

"Set, I never knew…" She does not finish her sentence as her gaze catches mine. Her eyes go wide, and she jumps up and backs into the corner. Afraid. She is scared *of me*.

"Ok, Mal. You saw her. Now it's time to go back to my chambers," Set breaks the silence.

"Olive, please. I did not mean to. I was not myself. I love you, my Olive." But she says nothing in return. Tears stream down her beautiful face as Set closes the door on me.

Chapter 7: Olive

It's HIM…Malsumis. My heart feels like it is going to beat out of my chest. I jump from the chair I am sitting in and I back into the closet corner, trying to put as much distance as I can between us. He says he loves me, and he was not himself. What do I do with that? Run back to the male who not days ago literally killed me? What does it say about me that part of me wants to do precisely that?

After a few moments, Set comes back into the room, and I'm still frozen in the corner, trapped in my own head with warring thoughts.

"I am sorry, Olive. He only wished to see that you were okay."

"I'm just not ready to face him yet. I'm not sure when or if I will ever be ready."

"I understand. I want you to know that he has been to the underworld and back for you. He has been on his knees begging other gods to help save you. I have known Mal for as long as I can remember, and he has never acted in this manner. You have changed him."

"I don't know what to do with that at the moment, Set."

"You do not have to do anything with it until you are ready. I thought you should know. I will go back to Mal know and let you rest. You have been through much since you got here."

"Set, how long exactly have I been here?"

"Time is different in this realm. In the human realm, it has been a month. He leaves the room with me standing here like a stunned deer in headlights.

I have been gone for a month. My life just…gone. What do my friends think happened? Mark. He will know Malsumis did something. I have to see him, I have to let him know I am okay. I need to get back home. I stomp to the door and swing it open. Set and Malsumis turn quickly and stare at me and my abrupt entrance.
Malsumis and his stupid, sexy mouth speaks first.

"Olive, are you okay? Are you ill? Do you wish to speak to me?" he questions, almost begging.

"Set, I need to get back to my realm. Like now," I say, ignoring Malsumis.

"There is no way until after your coronation into the pantheon," Set answers.

"No, I need to go now. I have people who are missing me. I need to let them know I am okay."

"People like Mark?" Malsumis jealously asks. I turn to him and look him in the eyes,

"You do not get to ask me things like that anymore." My words hit their mark by the hurt look that comes across his face, and I almost regret the retort. Stay strong, Olive.

"It is impossible, Olive. Until you are at full power, traveling alone would drain you." Set interrupts the awkward moment.

"Unless I take her for a short visit," Malsumis speaks up.

"Why would I go anywhere with you? Set, could you take me?"

"It is too risky. You are not ready yet, Olive. Until Ra imbues you with your power, you are weak, Olive. You still could die," Set explains. Malsumis looks sick as he turns to me; he must not have known this fact.

"Well, at least I would have a say in how I die," I say quietly as I turn to go back to my room.

"Olive, please speak with me. I will do anything just to have you speak to me again." Malsumis begs following me.

"Fine! You will do anything?" I say, turning and almost running into Malsumis's broad, muscular chest.

"Yes, anything, my Olive," He says pleadingly, looking into my eyes.

"Go to Mark and tell him what happened to me. Let him know that I'm okay and I will be back when I can."

"You will go back to him?" Malsumis asks quietly.

"I can't stay here," I answer just as quietly. He looks at me with such sadness that it takes all the resolve I have not to pull him into me. I turn away so that I don't break. I reach for the door, and he interrupts me.

"I will go to him for you, Olive," Malsumis says sadly.

"Thank you," I answer as I go into my room and close the door behind me. Why do I feel guilty? HE literally killed me. Why do I feel such a pull to him still? I lean back against the door, my heart aching. I can hear the conversation from the other room.

"Who is this Mark?" Set asks.

"Olive's male friend."

"I thought you and she were together?"

"We are. He is just her friend." Malsumis quickly retorts.

"Like Eris was just your friend? She is still hanging around waiting for you to warm her bed again." Jealousy surges through me at Set's words.

"Mark is just Olive's friend. Eris can keep waiting. I have found my mate, and I will be with her."

"You know Eris is not one to be pushed aside so easily."

"I do not care about her, and I do not wish to speak about her anymore. I need to go back to the human realm and find Mark. Will you please continue to keep Olive safe?"

"You know I will. She is quite intelligent. I have quite enjoyed speaking with her."

"Set," Malsumis growled.

"Nothing more, Mal. I know she is yours." Set chuckles.

Eris? Eris, as in the Greek Goddess of Discord and Strife? If the mythologies are true, she is quite beautiful, and of course, she is his ex. Now I have to make it to my coronation and stay clear of the pissed off ex girlfriend. There is a knock on the door, and I open it slowly to see Set on the other side.

"Would you like a tour of my palace? I am sure you are tired of these rooms by now."

"Actually, I would love that," I say, smiling up at Set.

Chapter 8: Malsumis

Olive wants me to visit Mark, and of course, I will, but I most certainly do not want to. This male tried to take my girl away from me, and I have not forgotten this. I conjure some modern clothing and head out to find Mark.

I head to the museum where Olive and Mark work. I can sense he is there today. I walk up to the information desk and ask the woman there if I can speak with Mark.

"Sure, I will call him up right away." She phones him and then turns back to me.

"I have never seen you around. Are you new to the area? I would love to show you around," she says.

"No," I say, looking around for Mark.

"Oh, are you *with* Mark? I didn't realize he was seeing someone. I am so sorry."

"I am not with Mark." What is that supposed to mean? I thought he wanted Olive.

"Oh, I'm sorry. I guess I will just shut up before I really put my foot in my mouth."

"That would be preferable," I say. She just gawks at my bluntness.

At that moment, Mark walks up. When he sees me, his eyes narrow, and his anger is palpable. His hands go into fists at his sides before he addresses me.

"Follow me to my office," he says shortly.

We walk into his office, and I see there are two desks. He shared this room with Olive. The thought comes to me, and the guilt hits me like a ton of bricks. I look over to her side and see all her degrees and achievements hanging on the wall. All the pictures of her on archeological digs and with her friends. I ruined all of this for her.

"What did you do with her, you son of a bitch?" Mark growls at me as I take a seat on a small couch.

"I am here on her behalf to let you know she is okay."

"Where is she? What the fuck have you done?"

"She is safe with my friend. I made a mistake, but it has been corrected." I stand to leave. Mark stands in front of the door, challenging me.

"What mistake?"

"What does it matter? Olive is mine, not yours. She will never be yours." I snap at him.

"You don't think I know that? I never planned on Olive. I am…it doesn't matter. Where is she? I want to see her."

"You cannot. Not yet anyway."

"What do you mean, *not yet*?"

"An accident happened. I had to take her to my realm. She is well, but not as she once was. She is like me now."

"What accident? What do you mean like you?"

"When she freed me…I was out of control. Not myself."

"Speak plainly and tell me what happened to Olive." He demands on the verge of tears.

"I killed her."

Whatever restraint he has breaks, and he comes at me. He lands several good punches before I knock him off of me.

"STOP!" I command, "If you were anyone else, under any other circumstance, I would already have dealt with you. Do not push me."

"Or what will you kill me like Olive?" he sneers. He walks to the couch and sinks down onto it, leaning forward with his head in his hands.

"Believe me, if I were in control of myself, it would not have happened," I say somberly.

"Yeah, keep telling yourself that. I have seen what you are capable of firsthand. I tried to warn her, but she was so adamant that you would never hurt her. I should have done more to keep her safe."

"When she can, Olive plans on coming to see you. I have fulfilled my promise to her to see you."

"Wait," Mark gets up, goes to his desk, and pulls out an envelope, "Can you give this to her?"

"What is it?"

"It is something just for Olive to see. Something I should have given her sooner."

"Fine, I will do this for her." I turn and leave him standing behind his desk with tears in his eyes.

Chapter 9: Olive

"How did you know who Mal was to free him?" Set asks as we walk down the cool stone hallway.

"My friend and I researched, and I had a contact from another museum who helped me piece things together."

"If you could not see him, how did you know he was there?"

"I could feel him, and I could see him in my dreams."

"You are a dream walker?"

"No, I always assumed his power allowed him to join my dreamstate."

"No, only a dreamwalker can do that. You were powerful even as a human. Interesting. I must tell my father so that he can properly assign you."

"Assign me?"

"We all have something that we are over. Like I am Chaos."

"Oh, I understand."

We enter Set's temple. The light is dim here, filtering through narrow slits in the walls. The smell is sharp, like the mix of incense and something metallic. Massive pillars flank the walkway and are adorned with hieroglyphs. These aren't the graceful lines like in Hathor's temple; these are angular and forceful, almost aggressive. In front of me is a mural of Set holding a storm. He isn't holding it to stop it, though; he is controlling it. He is not just chaos. He controls it, just like Malsumis. A chill moved through me, not the kind from the cold but the kind from knowing.

"Are you cold?" Set asks, noticing the shiver.

"No, I just never thought I would ever see anything like this in person. It is all surreal."

"I imagine this must be too much to take in. Do you need to rest?"

"No, I am okay. Actually, I can't remember the last time I slept."

"As gods, we do not need to sleep regularly."

"Malsumis did, though."

"He must have chosen to do so." He left the rest unsaid because of me. Malsumis slept so he could be with me. A stab of longing hit my chest.

"Oh, what do we have here?" a female voice cooed. I turned to see one of the most beautiful females I have ever seen. Her hair falls in dark, night waves down her back, adorned with a thorny crown of red gemstones. Her green eyes are sharp and burning through me as she looks at me like we are playing a game I didn't realize I was a part of. There is no warmth in them toward me. "Eris, not this one. She is Malsumis's." I went to protest, but Set looks at me sternly.

"Do you think so little of me? Do you share her, too?" she purrs, running a finger down Set's arm. I look up at him, shocked.
He shrugs. SHRUGS!

"No. She is Mal's. Eris, you know this. Why are you here again?"

"I want to speak with her. So, you think you can handle Mal?"

"I have done well so far," I say defiantly, earning a chuckle from Set.

"Such an attitude. Watch it, girl, you have no idea who you are talking to."

"Actually, I do. I just don't care." I sass back.

"Eris, it is time you leave," Set says, breaking us up.

"Are you kicking me out of your temple?"

"Yes, you have been warned to stay away from Olive, but refusing to do so, it is time for you to go." Eris leaves with a huff, and Set and I are left alone again in his temple.

"No one ever speaks that way to her besides Mal and me," Set says

"Well, maybe it's time someone did."

"Maybe it is," Set says with a laugh, "I believe we need to go see my father."

"Ra. We are going to see Ra?" I ask in awe.

"Oh gods, don't fawn over him like that; he will get a big head." Set laughs again.

"I mean, how can I not, Set! I totally fangirled over you at first, too."

"It's a shame you're Mal's or else I would keep you myself." Set winks. "Come on, hold my hand and let's go."

We arrive in Ra's temple, and I have to squint at the sudden change in light. The entire room is bathed in light, not from the sun but from something older, something divine. Heat pressed into my skin, not painfully or suffocating but warm and soothing. Tall golden columns etched in hieroglyphs rose like sunbeams captured in stone. At the center of the room, Ra stands from his throne. Standing before me is the most terrifyingly beautiful male. He stood as tall as Malsumis's seven feet at least with deep, shimmering obsidian skin. Each line of his body is carved with power and undeniable authority. His golden eyes meet mine, like two suns burning into my gaze. He sees me. All of me. My doubt.
My love. My longing. My defiance.

"You stand in the light by an accident, but not by accident, Olive. Welcome home." He speaks to me. My knees bend, not voluntarily but by instinct. He steps to me and stops a breath away, each movement controlled and absolute, "You still are angry?"

"Yes. Malsumis killed me. Everyone keeps saying it was an accident, but what am I supposed to do with that? Just forgive him and act as if nothing happened?" I blurt out. His eyes narrow.

"You have already forgiven him, Olive. Why live with anger? You could be happy right now. Leave these human feelings behind. Allow yourself to let go and enjoy your new life."

"I will take your words into consideration," I say, which earns me a loud laugh from him.

"I like you. Mal chose well. Now, what brings you two here today?" Ra asks as he puts a hand on me to rise.

"I know Olive has to go through coronation, but I thought you should know that I believe that as a human, she already processed dreamwalker power," Set explains.

"Brilliant!" Ra's voice booms, "Tell me, how did you realize this, Olive?"

"I thought it was Malsumis's power, but I guess it was me. When we slept and were touching, we could enter a dream state, and I could see and interact with him there. It is partly how I figured out who he was."

"Yes, this is good. Thank you for bringing this to my attention. Is there anything else?" Ra asks, his eyes never leaving mine.

"No, Father. We will leave you now." Set responds quickly.

"Thank you. It was nice to meet you." Smooth Olive.

"The pleasure was all mine, my dear." Ra lifts my hand to his lips.

Set grabs my other hand, and we go back to his room. When we get there, Malsumis is there pacing. Obviously, not happy that we were gone.

Chapter 10: Malsumis

I travel back to Set's rooms, and there is no sign of Set or Olive anywhere. I do not like this. He was supposed to keep her safe in these rooms until I came back. I walk out and stalk through the halls searching for them. I get to his temple and sense that they had been there. So had Eris. If she did something to Olive…no, Set would not have let anything happen. Where in the hell did he take her? I go back to his rooms and wait. The envelope Mark gave me is burning a hole in my pocket. What does it contain? Will it hurt Olive? Will it take her further from me? I begin to pace, my anger and anxiety increasing by the second. Suddenly, Olive and Set appear holding hands. My look must be murderous because Set quickly lets go.

"We went to see Father, Mal. Olive explained that you could visit each other's dreams, and we believe she is a dreamwalker. I thought that may aid Father in assigning her," Set says promptly.

"I see. I sensed you two and Eris in the temple." I try to speak calmly.

"She was there, but Olive handled her," Set explained. I looked at Olive.

"She is just another mean girl. I have dealt with her kind before," she says with a shrug, "Did you find Mark?"

"Yes. I explained what happened. He was upset, but he gave me something for you." I give her the envelope, and she tucks it into her dress.

"I promised you I would let you speak with me, so let's go," Olive says, gesturing to her room. I waste no time and go in before she changes her mind. We sit in the chairs near the bookcases.

"My Olive, please know I did not mean for this to happen. When my powers were freed, they came flooding back, and I momentarily lost control of myself. I believe that in that moment, my body thought I was back in the moment I was trapped. I do not know how to make this right. I love you. You are my mate. I have always felt the pull to you, and now I know it was the bond. I know you feel it too. Maybe not as strongly as me since you are not at full power yet, but you feel it, right?"

"Yes," she whispers. I allow myself to relax a little.

"Olive, tell me what I can do to fix us?"

"I honestly don't know. Everyone keeps saying it was an accident, but I'm struggling to come to terms with it. I died

Malsumis. When I close my eyes, I see you grabbing my throat. I feel the darkness grabbing me, trying to drag me back. You don't know what this is like. This isn't like me kissing Mark. My whole life was stolen away from me. My hopes, dreams, plans. Everything is gone, and you're the reason for that. So tell me, how am I supposed to get over this?"

"I do not know, my Love. I do know that I am going to be here by your side to do anything you need, though. If you need me to hold you, I will. If you need to tell me all of the horrible things I have done every day, then I will be here to listen. I am yours, Olive, and I am going nowhere." I reach out and caress her cheek, and for a second, she lets me before she pulls away.

"I'm not ready yet."

"I understand."

"Can I have some time alone to read what Mark sent?"

"Of course. I will be in Set's room if you need me."

I leave Olive sitting in her chair, opening the letter Mark sent. Jealousy spreads throughout me as I close the door. I know I do not deserve to feel that way, but I cannot help it. He has done nothing wrong to her. What if she chooses to go to him after her coronation? What if she decides to spend the rest of his life with him? It has been known to happen. I could dispose of him, but that would drive her further away. I will have to accept whatever role in her life that she allows me.

"How did it go?" Set asks from his table where he is eating.

"As good as can be expected. She is not ready to be with me again." I say, taking a seat.

"Father said she already has forgiven you, so that is a good start," Set says casually.

"She did not say that to me." I look at him, surprised to hear that.

"She is not ready to admit it," he surmises.

We hear commotion from Olive's room, Set and I look at each other and then hurry to her door. I rush in and see Olive crumpled on the floor in the middle of the room, sobbing. She had pushed the contents of her dining table to the floor and collapsed in the center of the mess. In her hand is the letter that Mark sent her. I knew he would do something to hurt her; I should have ended him. I go to her and kneel beside her and wrap her in my arms. She leans into me and cries harder.

"What did he do? Tell me and I will…" I start.

"He did nothing! You did! You took everything from me! My friends, everything I worked so hard for. You took my life!" She screams at me, pushing me away.

"Mal, maybe you should go. I will clean up and sit with her." Set suggests.

"No. I will not leave her. You can stay, but I will not go. Never." I say forcefully. Olive looks up at me with a mix of emotions on her face.

Set and I clean up the mess and sit in the chairs while Olive continues to mourn what her life was like. What it could have been. When she quietens, I go to her and pick her up. She is too exhausted to fight me, so she allows me to carry her to bed, and she falls asleep clutching the letter.

<u>Chapter 11</u>: Olive

My Girl,

I never could have imagined myself writing this letter to you. Yet not a single part of it feels wrong. Honestly, nothing has ever felt more right in my life.

I have spent most of my life knowing exactly who I am. When we first became best friends, I confided in you that I was gay because that is the truth I have known. Then, you happened. Not in a way that confused me, but in a way that expanded me. I realized love, for me, is not about a label. It is about the person. You are my person.

You have become the one that I love in the deepest, truest way I have ever known, not just as a friend, Olive. This is not just some connection. I genuinely feel that you are my soulmate. I long for you. Emotionally. Spiritually. Even romantically.

I don't want to tiptoe around this anymore. I am in love with you. Entirely. Fully. Unconditionally. I want you, Olive. All of you.

You have made me feel things I never thought possible, not by changing me but by seeing me, all of me. You love me with such clarity that I couldn't help but fall for you. You are my softness in this hard world. You are my calm. You are the person I want beside me in every chapter of my life.

I don't know where this path will lead us, but I want to walk it with you in any way that you will let me. No matter what the world says, this is real love, Olive. I know you love HIM too. I can live with that, as long as I have a place in your heart and by your side.

Forever Yours,

Mark

I can't breathe. Mark loves me. What am I supposed to do? I feel it too. That quiet ache, seemingly impossible love. I never let myself feel it before, knowing there was no chance of it being reciprocated. Now this changes everything. Right? I thought I had chosen. I chose Malsumis. I feel a strong pull to him, and when I am with him, even now, I know that is where I am supposed to be. He has seen every version of me. Rage. Ruin. Radiance. He has stayed through it all. I may deny it to his face right now, but deep down, I know we are meant for one another. But Mark. Mark haunts me like a song stuck in my head. He is my best friend. He is gentle, patient, supportive, and kind. He is impossible not to love. Am I in love with him, too? How am I supposed to choose? I'm breaking.

I stand up and begin to pace as my anxiety builds. Tears start to stream down my face. My anxiety is replaced by anger. I am angry that Malsumis took my choices from me. I am angry that Mark didn't tell me sooner. I am just furious. I begin to throw the contents of a nearby table to the floor. I know it was loud, and someone will come, but I don't care. My knees collapse beneath me, and I land on the floor sobbing.

Malsumis rushes in and kneels in front of me. I don't fight him when he pulls me in and lets me cry into his chest. Being near him feels right. I lose myself in his familiar warmth and let him comfort me until he threatens Mark. I push Malsumis away. How dare he think that this is Mark's fault? It was HIM who did this to me!

While I continue to sit and cry, he and Set clean my mess and wait patiently for me to calm down. True to his earlier words, Malsumis doesn't leave when I push him away or yell at him. He waits for me to calm down from exhaustion and picks me up. Again, I let him comfort me. He puts me onto my bed, and it doesn't take long for sleep to come for me.

At first, I'm drifting in the darkness and begin to panic, but then I realize that it is not entirely dark here. I'm not in the shadows again. All around me are distant stars with wisps of silver clouds woven in the tapestry of night. This is a dream realm. A warm light catches my attention, and I turn to it. A sense of longing washes over me. The closer I get, a figure forms; it's Malsumis. A garden forms around us. A mudbrick wall surrounds us, with vines of deep green climbing up it in spirals and pale white lotus flowers growing atop them. There are rectangular pools of water before us that are reflecting the constellations above in their calm, dark waters.

He is sitting in front of the fountain in the center of the garden. Palm trees that circle the fountain sway in the breeze as I approach. I silently sit beside him and notice that he is holding something in his hand. It is the letter Mark wrote. He looks up, but not at me.
Instead, he faces the night sky.

"Do you feel the same way about him?" A tear slides down the side of his face.

"I...I don't know. I didn't expect him to feel this way. Things are different now anyway. I can't go back to the life I had before. So even if I do feel something, it would never work."

"You have years that you can live the life you had in your realm before you would need to move on. He is mortal. It could work."

"What are you doing?" I turn my entire body to look at him.

"Giving you a way out. Giving you a way to get far from me if that is what you wish."

"Malsumis, I don't know what I want, but I do know that I want it to be my choice. I have had so many of those taken my whole life, and it stops now. I will be in control of my future."

"I understand. I will not stand in your way as you make those decisions. Even if it is being with someone else."

"I am just so confused. I am angry. I am hurt. I am mourning a life I thought I was going to have. I just need some time."

"Of course you do. I will not rush you. I will be here."

We sit in silence, staring into the sky for a long while. I reach over and take his hand into mine. He immediately stills as if he will scare me away if he moves. After several moments, he raises it to his mouth and kisses the top of my hand. We look into each other's eyes, and then I wake up alone in my bed in Set's rooms.

Chapter 12: Malsumis

I sit up in Set's garden after Olive visited my dream. I did not mean to read the letter, and I wish I had not. Olive dropped on the floor as she slept, and when I bent to retrieve it, I saw what it said. Gods, I love her, but maybe she would be better off with Mark. He said that he was okay with her being with me as well as with him. Could I ever do that, too? For her, I may. It would have to be her decision. I will not push her to be with me after what I have done to her.

"Aw, what is wrong, Mal? You look absolutely miserable." Eris says teasingly as she runs a finger across my shoulders.

"I see you are not listening to Set and staying away."

"Just because you do not want me to warm your bed does not mean he doesn't still enjoy me." She states matter-of-factly.

"So why are you here, bothering me?"

"We both know he is not the one that I want, Mal." She steps in front of me while I am sitting on a bench, putting her hands on my face, "You know we had fun together."

"Eris, that is enough." I grab her hands and go to push her away.

"Oh dear. Hello, Olive." Eris feigns a remorseful tone. I turn and look to see Olive standing in the garden's entrance, wide eyed and tearful.

"Olive, this is not what it looks like," I call, pushing Eris back.

"Nope, you're all good. It's totally fine. I'm just leaving," Olive says, trying to sound nonchalant.

"No, Olive. Please wait." I call after her. I catch up and touch her arm. She spins around quickly.

"What do you want? Go back to her, Malsumis. We aren't together, right?"

"In my mind, we are together, Olive."

"That sure as fuck didn't look like it." She closes her eyes and takes a breath, "Look, I don't have a right to be upset, I guess. I am the one who doesn't know what she wants. I can't blame you for seeking comfort."

"Olive, I swear that is not what that was…"

"It really doesn't matter. I have to go." She opens Set's door and disappears behind it. He warded his rooms to let her in? He

has never done that for anyone. Jealousy spreads through me
like wildfire.

Chapter 13: Olive

I lean against the door and, with my eyes closed, knowing that Malsumis is standing behind it and unable to enter. It shouldn't bother me, right? I am the one saying we aren't together. What do I care if he talks to his ex? Even as I think it jealously surges through me.

"I am guessing Eris found Mal?" Set comments, interrupting my thoughts.

"How would you even know that?"

"She said she was going to find him before she left earlier."

"So you and she are still…a thing? Even though she wants Malsumis, too?"

"We have always just been together, the three of us. It doesn't bother me," he looks at me and gives a shrug, "As far as Mal goes, she has zero chance now."

"That isn't what it looked like in the garden."

"I assure you that what you saw was what Eris wanted you to see."

"It doesn't matter anyway. He can do whatever he wants. I don't care."

"Hmm. Sure." He lifts a brow to my lie.

"Anyway, what do you do for fun here?"

"Anything that you would in your realm. Any requests?"

"I really could go for a movie to get my mind off of everything."

"You got it."

✳✳✳

A couple of hours later, I have my head thrown back in laughter as Set and I are well into our comedy marathon. My cheeks ache from smiling so much. I can't remember the last time I smiled since all of this started.

"You have the most infectious laugh," Set chuckles.

"I hope that is a compliment!"

"Oh, it is. I could grow used to hearing it…" He is interrupted by a hard knock at the door.

Set opens the door, and Malsumis stomps in, looking dangerous. The air shifts. It's heavy, charged. Malsumis's eyes go from Set to me, searching every inch of the scene. Our laughter still lingers in the air as Set straightens.

"Olive and I were watching movies to help pass the time."

"Apparently," Malsumis answers, his voice sharp.

"We were just…" I start.

"Laughing. I heard."

Set glances between us and mutters something about his father needing something and quickly went out the door. The moment Set leaves, Malsumis's gaze doesn't soften.

"Having fun?"

"We were just watching movies and talking."

"Seemed like more than that."

"What does it matter? We aren't together." I force a shrug.

"Olive, you are mine. You don't get to laugh and smile at him like that." His gaze drops to my lips. My heart hammers in my chest as he closes the space between us.

"Why? Because I am yours?" I sass, albeit quietly.

"Exactly." His look is raw, desperate. He lowers enough that his lips are almost brushing mine, and I have to fight the urge to pull him closer by his shirt.

The door swings open, and Set steps in and clears his throat. The moment is lost, but Malsumis's eyes stay on me, dark and lingering.

"This is not over," he breathes.

"Father, is ready for Olive's coronation. He requests our presence in his temple."

Chapter 14: Olive

We arrive at Ra's temple, and two priestesses immediately whisk me away to a private room to dress for the coronation. My first instinct is to reach for Malsumis as they lead me away. He reassures me that everything will be okay, and I instantly calm down. I hate that he has that control over me. Or maybe I don't really hate it…my head is so fucked up.

The room we enter is much like the rest of Ra's temple, bright and gold. The dress I am to wear is hanging in the center of the room. The gown is glowing faintly in the torchlight. It looks as if it has been woven from the night sky. The black sequins shimmer like captured stars. A collar of gold filigree secures the plunging halter neckline, and the open sides of the gown are held by delicate gold chains framing the waist and hips.

"I can't wear this. There is no way it will fit." I remark to the priestesses.

"Ra himself created it. It will fit."

When I slip the dress on, I am shocked to find it not only fits but also feels like it's claiming me. I look in the mirror and don't recognize who is looking back at me. I am me, but different. I feel confident for the first time in…well, ever. I wish Mark could see me like this. Feelings of guilt and longing stab my chest.

The priestesses show me to the temple's main doors and instruct me to stand and wait until the doors open, and then walk down the aisle to Ra. I take a deep breath to try to calm my nerves. The golden doors open, and the heavily incensed air curls around me. I walk down the aisle that is covered in a river of silken petals and let the swell of chanted hymns vibrate through my bones.

The gods upon their thrones line both sides of the aisle. Some watch with warm pride, others are unreadable. As I reach Ra, I see Malsumis and Set on either side of the aisle, waiting and watching, giving their silent support. Malsumis's gaze heats as he looks me over, and heat pools in my stomach.

Ra rises from his throne. His voice rolls like thunder, yet carries like gentleness of rain.

"From the first spark, I have watched the world turn. I have seen mortals rise and fall. Mortal no longer. By the will of the divine, you are now home, Olive. Today, I crown you, not as a gift, but as a truth long written in the stars. Take this crown, forged in my own light. Wield it as you have your own heart, fiercely, wisely, and without fear.”

With a smile beautiful enough to halt the heavens, Ra places a delicate crown of molten gold and threads of moonlight on my head. The moment it settles, the temple explodes with light, and my heartbeat slows, changes. My skin glows faintly from within, and the gods bow in acknowledgement that I am one of them now.

Everything fades to a blur. The gods all come, offer greetings and welcomes, and then leave. Malsuis stands back and watches intently until everyone is gone. He walks to me and kneels before me.

“I am forever yours, Olive. You are the only goddess I have ever and will ever worship. You are MY goddess, my equal, my only. I kneel to no other but you.” He looks up at me, and I brush his hair from his face. He closes his eyes and leans into my touch.

We stay like this for several moments.

“I forgive you, Malsumis. I think I forgave you a while ago. I just don’t know where to go from here. I want to go back to my life. I want to salvage what I can before it is too late. I just don't know what to do about us." I admit, and he stands facing me.

"I can go with you. We can be together, Olive."

"Part of me wants that more than anything."

"The other part wants Mark," he says in a hushed tone.

"Yes." There it is. I love Mark too. I want to give him a chance.

"I will always be waiting for you." Before I can respond, Malsumis is gone.

Chapter 15: Mark

It has been three months since I last saw Olive's face. Two, since that motherfucker came and told me he killed her and brought her back, since I gave him the letter I wrote to her. Nothing since then, and it has driven me crazy. I can't eat. I can't sleep. Is he keeping her from me? Does she not feel the same? Did I mean nothing to her?

I have covered for her at work by emailing from her account, letting HR know that she had a family emergency out of town and needed a leave of absence. I have been to her house, paid her bills, and repaired her broken windows. Every time, it is like a punch in the stomach. I am miserable without her.

I am in my kitchen making a sandwich for dinner when I hear a knock at the front door. I grab a knife to take with me because I am not expecting anyone, and it is highly unusual for someone to be at my door. I open the door.

It's HER. I am stunned. I can't breathe. After three long months, she is finally here. I drop my knife to the floor.

"What about me makes you males murderous?" She quips, breaking the silence.

"Olive," I whisper, afraid she is going to disappear.

She smiles, and it shakes me from my stupor. I close the space between us and pull her into my arms.

"I thought you were gone," I breathe against her hair.

"I was," she admits, curling her hands in my shirt, "The gods made a mistake if they thought I would leave you behind, though."

I lean back, look into her eyes, and see how the light in them has changed. There is a divine light to them, but when I look further, I see the woman I loved before. I will bend the heavens themselves to keep her with me.

I thought I knew what it was to love her.

I thought I knew what it was to want her.

I was wrong.

I reach for her like a man starved. My hands frame her face, and my lips claim hers, hungry, desperate, disbelieving she is real. She lets me press her back into the wall, our bodies molding together. I kick the door closed behind us and lead her to my bedroom.

"Are you sure?" I ask, praying she is.

"Yes," she breathes as she leans in to kiss my neck.

That is all I need to hear. Our hands are everywhere, frantic. She is about to show me something dangerous, and I am not sure I will survive it. I slide her gown from her shoulders, kissing my way as I go. Her skin is warm and has a faint glow in the moonlight. If I didn't know that she was a literal goddess now, I would miss it. Then again, when it comes to her, I never miss anything.

She runs her finger down my chest, and I feel a heat sinking into me, running through my blood. Every nerve feels like it is being struck by lightning, and my breath catches.

"Breathe," she breathes, gods…her voice. I have missed her.

I did as I was told, but barely as she began to kiss my neck. Whatever mortal sense I have shatters, as heat rolls into me in waves, pulling sounds from my throat I didn't realize I could make. I want to memorize every sound she makes, every curve of her body. I cling to her hips as she lowers herself on me. She moves slowly at first, every shift of her hips sending sparks of pleasure through me. She keeps going, increasing her speed until I am gripping her like a man drowning. As the pressure builds, I meet her with my own thrusts. I can't tell where she ends, and I begin. We build the pace until we come together, violently, like the sun itself ripped through me and left nothing behind but raw bliss and her name. When I come down, I can still feel thrumming through my bones.

She looks at me, and her lips curve into a smile like she is claiming a victory.

"You're mine?" As if she has to ask.

"Always." My voice is wrecked with emotion. I have been hers for a long time now.

She lies curled up against my chest, her soft, platinum hair spilling over my shoulder, the warmth of her skin seeping into mine. How many nights have I dreamt of this very moment? This is better than all of them. For the first time in months, I feel whole and happy.

"Does it scare you, what I have become?" She asks softly.

"No. I am only scared of losing you." I tighten my arm around her and breathe in her scent.

"I didn't come back to leave you," she whispers, almost too low to hear.

Her words sink into me. Is it possible that she loves me as I do her? I hope that is true, but honestly, I will accept anything she offers to be at her side. I close my eyes, resting my chin on her head, letting the quiet blanket around us. The world outside could keep turning. All I care about is the woman in my arms. Nothing else matters.

Chapter 16: Olive

For the first time since that day Malsumis took my life, I actually feel happy. I feel like this is where I need to be, in Mark's arms. The bed is warm beneath us. The sheets are tangled, and the night air is brushing over my bare skin. His chest is rising and falling under my cheek, and each breath he takes loosens something in me that I didn't realize was wound so tightly. For the first time since I was brought back into immortality, I actually feel alive. It has nothing to do with the gods that brought me back; it has everything to do with being in his arms.

A pang of guilt hits me. I searched for Malsumis before I left, but he didn't want to be found. I never wanted to hurt him, but how can I be with him after what happened? Right now, I just can't be.

I love him, but I love Mark, too.

Mark's soft snores let me know that he has drifted off. I touch his temple and send soothing dreams through to him. He looked so depressed, not like my Mark when he opened the door to me earlier. I could have popped in without knocking, but I didn't want to scare him. When I saw him, my heart broke. He didn't deserve any of this. Yet, he has been paying this price for my mistake in trusting Malsumis.

As for me, I have some unfinished business to take care of now that I am back and at full power. I close my eyes and let myself drift off to my dreamscape. I let the darkness surround me as I think of the people I most need closure with. My grandmother.

It doesn't take long to find her. She is dreaming of being back in the house, minus me, of course. I slip in and stand behind her.

"Hello, Grandmother." She spins around to meet me and looks me up and down in that demeaning way she always does.

"What are you doing here? You're not allowed here," she spits.

"Oh, I beg to differ. I am allowed wherever I want to be now." I dissolve the space she created, leaving us surrounded by a dark void. She is completely alone, except for me. She has no choice but to face me, the ultimate consequence of her malice.

"Stop this! Take me back, I'm scared!" She screeches into the darkness.

"No, it is far past time that you face me, Grandmother. Far past time that you feel the isolation and emptiness I felt all those years with you." Her eyes widen in shock and fear.

"Olive, please don't hurt me," she cries.

"Why not? You never minded hurting me. Telling me things like I was going to be big enough to be in a side show attraction, letting those men do whatever they wanted to me, and then calling me a liar, even making fun of me when I came to you for help. Oh, what about the times you would put your hands on me, pull my hair? So tell me why I should spare you?"

"I'm your blood, Olive. I'm your family." That makes me laugh.

"Blood? Yes, but it never mattered to you. Why would it matter to me? Family? Never."

"Please, Olive, don't kill me."

"Kill you? Oh no, I'm not going to do that." She releases a breath she was holding, "I am going to let you have a taste of the fear and isolation I felt all of those years." I turn to leave.

"Olive, don't leave me here." She demands and reaches for my arm. My power flares and burns her hand.

"DO NOT TOUCH ME!" I command. She shrinks back with her eyes full of shock and fright. "You do not get to hurt me again. You will know a fraction of the pain and loneliness I have felt my entire life with you. Now, I am done here for now. I have an actual family to get back to." With that, I leave her standing in the void, all alone, just like she left me all those years.

I wake up just before Mark. I spend a moment just looking at him. The morning light is falling across his face, highlighting his warm toned skin and a faint stubble on his sculpted jaw. He has that effortless charm even when he sleeps. His thick, dark blonde hair is tousled and almost in his eyes. I brush it away softly. Before I move my hand away, I lightly trace the side of his face with my fingertips.

"Mmm, if you don't stop, I am going to want round two."

"I would be okay with that," I softly chuckle.

Before I realize it, he flips us over, and is on top of me. His hand finds my jaw and tilts my face up toward him, and then his lips are on mine. Gods, he tastes good. Gods, he feels good. My breath hitches as he lines up with me, and that sound alone sends something primal through him. He doesn't kiss me gently; he claims me. His mouth is hot and searching, his tongue parting my lips in a demand that sends my pulse thundering.

My nails scrape along his back in answer to his slow, deliberate thrusts. He moves his lips to the column of my neck, and I moan.

"Fuck, Olive. You make the most beautiful sounds when I'm inside you."

More heat pools low in my body, and my knees weaken even more. As he picks up his pace, his mouth finds mine again. Hot, insistent, tasting of hunger and possession. He trails back down to my collarbone and bites hard enough to elicit a gasp from my lips.

"Say you're mine, Olive."

"Yours. I'm yours."

My power surges around us, but it is still nothing compared to the raw consuming fire of his touch. His thrusts are becoming faster and more erratic as we both near coming. Our bodies move together in a frantic rhythm as we come together.

I look up at Mark from where I am lying on his chest. He is already looking at me.

"What?" I giggle.

"Did you mean it? Did you really mean you're mine?"

"Yes. I love you. Not even death could keep me from you."

He smiles, and I know I am exactly where I need to be. Although in the back of my conscience, I know there will be a time when I have to choose between him and Malsumis.

Chapter 17: Mark

"I need to go to my house to make sure everything is okay. I am sure that my power has been disconnected because I haven't paid for three months. There are probably burst pipes and all sorts of headaches to deal with. Plus, I need some clothes. I can't exactly wear my gown or go naked everywhere." Olive explains over breakfast.

"First off, you can stay here and stay naked, and that would be fine with me," I give her a wink, and she giggles. I love that sound. "Second, we need to talk about some things about your house and about what you have been through."

"Oh no, that sounds bad."

"It's not bad. I promise. I just want us to understand what the other has been through."

"Do you want me to meet you for lunch? I am sure I don't have a job now."

"I texted Nicole that I won't be in today. You're stuck with me for the day." I lift her hand and kiss it, "and you're not out of a job. I emailed Nicole from your email and got you a leave of absence for a family emergency out of state."

"How did you know I would be back?"

"I knew he was involved, and I thought that he wouldn't let anything happen to you. So I knew you would be back. Plus, what was I going to say to the authorities? Oh, yes, Officer, a god kidnapped my best friend."

"I never thought he would hurt me. When I freed him, he lost control, and his mind went back to when he was trapped. It really was an accident. It has happened to other gods, too." "You truly believe it was an accident?" She nods and looks to the floor.

"Then why are you here? Why not stay with him?"

"I forgive him, but when I look at him, I remember everything I went through. His hand around my throat, the shadows wrapping themselves around me, pulling me into darkness. Clawing my way out of the veil."

The more she speaks, the more furious I become. He put her through this and claims he loves her? How can she forgive him?

"I'm glad I got in those punches when he came to see me."

"You did what?" She says, surprised.

"I guess he didn't say anything because it would make him look bad if a mortal got one over on him." I chuckled.

"Considering his feelings about humans, I would say so."

"He liked you, so not all humans."

"He only liked me as a human because he felt the pull." She takes my hand, "He is my mate. That is why we felt that pull to each other. Yes, I still have feelings for him, and I don't know what will happen with that. I have feelings for you, too. I do know what I want from those feelings, though."

"What do you want, Olive?"

"You. This. Us. Just as I felt the pull to HIM, I have felt drawn to you from the beginning. I never allowed myself to think anything of my feelings because I thought there was no way you felt the same way." She admits.

"I want us too. I have wanted you from the moment we met. I didn't let myself feel that at first. I was so convinced that I was supposed to feel a certain way because that was how I knew myself. You changed everything, Olive. I knew in Salem that I was falling for you. I meant every word in my letter. I'm here no matter what you choose to do. If that means you're with him too, then we will navigate that."

She leans into me and kisses me gently. I pull her close and deepen the kiss. I will never get tired of kissing her.

"If you keep kissing me like this, we will never leave the house," she teases.

"You assume I want to leave the house if you are here." I tease back, and she gives me a soft push.

"Come on, let's go. I really need my own clothes."

✳✳✳

We pull into her driveway, and I can feel her shift in mood. I can tell she is replaying the events of three months ago in her head.

She explained to me that in the realm she was in, time passed differently. So it only seemed like a few days to her. I am still trying to wrap my head around everything she has been through. Plus, the fact that she is a literal goddess, a dream goddess to be exact.

"Don't worry about your car. I came over and started it every couple of days to make sure it would still run for you." I brought it up, trying to shake her out of her sadness.

"Thank you so much! I'm surprised that it didn't get repossessed, honestly."

"I may have paid the payment so that didn't happen." I fess up.

"Mark, thank you! I will pay you back."

"No, you won't. You being here with me is enough." She leans into a quick kiss before we get out and head into the house.

"I can't believe my power is still on!" She exclaims as we walk inside.

"I may have paid that too," I admit. She turns quickly to face me.

"Okay, fess up, what all did you do? I seriously owe you."

"You owe me nothing. I did everything because I love you. I didn't want you to worry about anything when you came back. I kept the bills up, repaired the windows that were broken, and…" I trail off, not wanting to say what else I did.

"What else, Mark?"

"There was blood on the carpet. Not much, but I cleaned it so you wouldn't see it when you got back." I stop holding back the tears that I have had since she showed up at my door last night.
She pulls me in and holds me close.

"It's okay. I promise I felt no pain. The blood was from the exchange he made to save me."

"Olive, it's not okay. You died. You are immortal now. I lost you, and now what do I have to offer you? I am nothing." She pulls away and holds my face in her hand. She looked me in the eyes.

"Nothing? Mark, you are everything. I came back for you, nothing else. You. I love you."

"Say it again," I say softly.

"I love you, Mark. I always have."

My lips meet hers, desperate to feel her close again.

"I love you, Olive," I say into our kiss. I feel her smiling in response.

My phone begins to ring in my pocket, and I hit the side button to send it to voicemail. I lead Olive to the couch and lay her down across it. I hover over her, kissing down her throat, and let my teeth graze the spot that makes her arch into me. My phone rings again, and I send it to voicemail again. Olive rakes her nails down my back hard enough to make me growl into her collarbone. My phone rings again.

"You should probably answer that," she says. I grab the phone.

"Hello?" I answer shortly.

"OH NO, you didn't just answer like that after you sent me to voicemail twice!" Jennifer sassily replies.

"I'm busy. What is it?" I nuzzle into Olive's neck, trailing her throat with quiet kisses.

"Ew, I can hear that. Look, are you still coming to The Loft tonight?"

"Shit, I totally forgot."

"Mark, this is for you! You have been moping ever since Olive left. Although it sounds like you have found someone to pass the time with," Jennifer fusses.

Olive lightly pushes me up and signals that she wants to go.
All I want to do is finish what we just started, but I will do
anything for this woman.

"Fine, I will be there."

"Good. We are just worried about you, Marky." She knows I
can't stand that name.

"I know, Jenny," I counter.

"Ugh, I will see you later." She hangs up, and I laugh.

"Yay, I can't wait to see the girls! I have to go get ready."
Olive hops up and heads towards the stairs, "Fancy a shower?"

She didn't even need to ask that. I chase her up the stairs as
she laughs.

Chapter 18: Olive

A night out with friends is exactly what we need to get our minds off everything heavy. I walk up to The Loft with my hand laced in Mark's. Music is spilling from the open doors, and laughter and conversations from all around are carried through the cool April night. I replaced my flowing gown with curve hugging jeans and a loose top that sways with every step. To everyone else, I am just someone out for a night of fun. Only Mark knows better.

"OMG, OLIVE!" Candy calls out. Jennifer turns to see us and smiles widely.

"We have missed you, girl! How does it feel to be back in civilization? It must have been torture without cell service for three months!" Jennifer chats.

"It feels so good to be back. I have missed you guys so much. Let's go have some fun!" I answer back.

We claim the back corner booth in the bar area and order some drinks. We chat and joke around for a while before Jennifer dares me to dance with her. I laugh, and some strangers turn and look at me like they are entranced. Goddess Olive has some admirers.

I join Jenn on the dance floor and let myself go. I sway my hips, raise my arms, moving in time with the beat. My eyes found Mark's from across the room, and I could feel the heat from his look. It wasn't long, and he was joining me. He slips behind me with his hands on my waist, pressing his body into mine and guiding mine to the music. On the surface, it was playful, but I know he was feeling the same fire I was.

We go back to our booth and sit close together, knees touching, our hands intertwined under the table.

"So…" Jennifer starts with a sly grin, "are we finally allowed to talk about the *obvious* thing going on here?

"FINALLY! I had money on this happening a long time ago!" Candy pipes in.

I laugh, my cheeks warming as I duck my head. My light, unguarded laughter gave me away, though. Mark just chuckled and gave my hand a little squeeze.

"The way you two looked at each other was painful. Do you know how many times we had to pretend not to notice?" Jennifer continues.

"Mark, you used to show up where she was and look after her like a lost puppy. We thought we were going to have to stage an intervention!" Candy went on.

"You're all ridiculous," he laughs, wrapping his arm around me and kissing my head.

"Ridiculously RIGHT!" Jennifer exclaims, and we all laugh.

I lift my gaze to him, and for a moment, I feel my power pulsing beneath my skin. All anyone else sees is me leaning into him and him looking at me like I am the only one in the room.

"To the worst kept secret in history, finally out in the open!" Jennifer toasts, and we just roll our eyes and laugh.

When we finally slip out into the crisp night air, I shoot Mark a sideways look.

"Lost puppy, huh?" I tease.

"I wasn't sneaking in everywhere you went. I just…happened to be there." He chuckles and pulls me close.

"Mmhm." I raise an eyebrow, "Staring at me across the room for months was what? A coincidence?"

"Research. Very thorough research," he says after pretending to think for a moment. That earns him a soft laugh meant just for him.

I playfully bump him with my hip.

"Well, your *research* wasn't very subtle. Apparently, everyone noticed."

"I can't help it. I am terrible at hiding my feelings for you." He leans in, his voice low enough that it makes my skin warm, "Besides, it worked, didn't it?"

"Maybe. I mean, you *did* look a little pathetic…" I smirk, feigning thoughtfulness. Before I can finish, he faces me and pulls me against him.

"Pathetic?" He mocks being wounded.

"Adorably so," I tease, curving my lips to a smile.

He kisses me then, quick, firm, and playful. His grin is wicked when he pulls back.

"Our friends were right about one thing."

"Oh, what was that?" I ask.

"I actually was following you around like a lost puppy. Only because you are the only one that I'd ever let lead me anywhere." It's my turn to kiss him then.

When I pull back, he brushes his thumb across my lower lip. The banter dissolves into something heavier, something that makes my pulse quicken.

"If you keep looking at me like that, we will never make it home," I say quietly.

"Good," he murmurs, leaning down, his lips ghosting mine. "I don't want to wait."

The kiss that follows is nothing like the teasing, playful ones we just shared. This one is deeper, hungrier. It is stealing the air from my lungs. I curl my hands into his shirt to anchor myself. He slips his other arm around me, pulling me fully against him. The world blurs, the cool night, the glow of the streetlights, the quiet rhythm of the passing cars; none of it exists beyond the heat of his mouth and the thrum of his heartbeat under my hand. When we finally break apart, he rests his forehead on mine.

"Anyone could see us," I managed to get out, though the way I am tracing his jaw with my fingers is betraying my lack of protest.

"Let them see us. I have waited long enough to have you like this." He smiles against my skin when his lips brush against my temple.

His hand slips into my hair, tilting my head back so he can take my mouth more fully. His tongue brushes mine in a way that makes my toes curl inside my shoes. His lips trail from my mouth to my jaw, down to the hollow of my throat. I gasp, and it is quickly swallowed as his mouth claims mine again. This kiss is reckless and hungry, like we have both been starving for this moment. A pair of passersby laugh as they walk past, but neither of us pulls away. Instead, he kisses me harder, as if he is daring the world, even the gods, to keep watching. I only smile against his lips before kissing him back just as fiercely, my hands curling into his hair, pulling him closer.

"We should go," I whisper against his lips when we finally pull apart.

"Not yet," he answers, stealing one more long, searing kiss beneath the streetlight.

Chapter 19: Olive

We barely get the door shut to his house when his hands find my waist, spinning back and pushing me into the wall with a thud. He pins my hands above my head, and then his mouth crashes down on mine.

"Mine." He whispers low and rough.

All the restraint he had at the bar and all the way home is gone, and all that is left now is pure hunger. I gasp into the kiss, and he swallows the sound greedily, pressing me deeper into the wall. He lets go of my arms so that he can roam over my body, settling his hands on the curve of my hips. My fingers fumble with the hem of his shirt, pulling it over his head with a frustrating urgency, earning me a low chuckle from him. The sight of his bare chest in the dim light makes my breath catch, but I have no time to linger. We quickly shed the rest of our clothes, then he lifts me with ease against the wall, and I wrap my legs around him instinctively. He lines up with me and slips into me with a devastatingly slow rhythm. His hand curls into my hair and pulls my head back to better access the column of my neck. He bites down. Then I let out a moan and am immediately rewarded with a growl from him and an increase in his pace. He slows again and then pulls out of me slowly. I whimper. He kneels in front of me.

"Put your leg on my shoulder, Olive," he demands, and of course, I oblige. "I am going to worship you, my goddess."

He uses his finger to enter me at a quick pace and makes slow swirls with his tongue around my clit. I am afraid I am about to combust at that alone. Gods, everything this man does feels divine. When he adds a second finger and crooks them just so, I begin to unravel and become a mewling mess. He growls into me, and that sends me over the edge. When I come, I see stars. I feel my powers surge and wrap us like a warm breeze. As I am coming down, he kisses his way back up my body.

"You taste divine. I could eat you for every meal," he says, his voice low. His teeth graze the base of my throat, and I moan.

"Knees. Now," he commands.

It sends shivers through me to hear him like this. He must see my reaction because his lips curl into a slow smile. I get on my knees in front of him and look up at him, waiting for his next instructions.

"Such a good girl," he says, looking down at me, taking my hair, and wrapping it around his hand. That statement had heat pooling between my legs. "Are you going to take me now, Olive?"

"Yes," I rasp.

"Do you like it when I tell you what to do? When I, a mortal, command you?"

"Yes." I REALLY like it.

"Take me in your mouth, Olive. Now."

I wrap my hands around him and his cock between my lips. I feel him tighten his grip on my hair, and he moans. That only feeds my enthusiasm as I take him deeper. He is so large, I know I can't take him fully. I gag, and that elicits another moan from him.

"Fuck that's it, baby." Those words do something to me, and I slip a hand between my legs. "Mmm, my girl is greedy. Get up and go to the couch, Olive."

When I do, Mark is behind me and bends me over the back of the couch. He lines up and enters me slowly.

"You're so wet, baby. You're ready to take me hard, aren't you?"

"Please, Mark."

He pulls out and thrusts in me hard. I am moaning immediately and loudly. That only fuels him and his pace. He reaches around and begins circling my clit with his fingers as he continues to fuck me.

"Come for me, Olive."

It is like a dam breaks, and I come, spasming around him. He follows behind me with a release of his own. He leans forward, trailing kisses up my spine.

"You have no idea what you do to me." He tells me.

"If it is a fraction of what you do to me, yes, I do."

We go to the bathroom, and Mark runs a bath for us. He gets me to lean back, and he washes my hair. Then he gets in, and we bathe each other. Never have I had this. Even though at one time I felt cherished with Malsumis, it wasn't like this, although I believe it could have been if… Even at the thought of his name, I feel a tug of guilt.

We lie in bed wrapped in one another. Mark is tracing idle circles along my bare shoulder. I lift my head and meet his gaze in the dim light. His green eyes are dark but unguarded. The way he is looking at me makes my throat tighten.

"You don't know what you have done to me, do you?" I ask.

"What's that?" He asks, his brows knitting as he brushes a thumb on my cheek.

"You have made me want to stay," I confess. "Here. Like this. With you."

"Then stay," he whispers, holding me like he is afraid I may slip away. "Forget gods, forget destiny. Just…stay."

My lips tremble into a smile, and I curl against him, listening to his steady heartbeat. For the first time, I let myself think that I might actually be able to belong to Malsumis *and* him.

Chapter 20: Malsumis

I disappear for a few days until I know Olive has gone back to her world. As much as I want her with me, she is struggling, and I need to let her go figure everything out. I will support her from afar.

"So what is your big dramatic plan to win her back?" Set asks.

"There is no dramatic plan. I have to wait for her to be ready to be with me."

"What if it takes a while?" Set keeps on with his questioning.

"Then I wait."

"What if she is with the human?"

"I know she is. She has to figure this out. As much as I dislike it, I must not push myself on her. I realize this."

"What if…" Set continues on before I interrupt him.

"Enough, Set. Why don't we do something to get my mind off my mate being with another male?"

"Well, typically, we would just incite a war or unleash a plague.

Oh, I got it, let's start a new cult. Those are always fun."

"None of those things remotely sounds enticing."

"You have changed, Mal. How can you be a god of chaos with no desire for chaos?"

"Find your mate, Set. Then we will talk."

"Let's go raid Hathor's wine cellars and get you drunk."

"That is the best idea you have had…ever." I could use a drink or thirty.

We sneak into Hathor's temple and gather more wine than the two of us could ever drink. We go back to Set's gardens and begin our night of revelry. It is not long before we are completely inebriated and reminiscing about our past.

"Do you remember when we stole Zeus's lightning bolt?" Set laughs.

"Your father was so proud, even though he had to smooth things over by taking Eris from Zeus's hair for all those years." I recount.

"Well, we did gain a partner in crime and uh, in other ways for a while."

"Don't remind me. You are more than welcome to keep her all to yourself." I groan.

"Oh, Mal, don't be like that. You know we have had our fun." Eris pouts.

"I knew better than to speak your name. You're always slithering around somewhere," I retort.

"Eris, not tonight," Set warns.

"Why, I just want to join in your little party. I promise I am just trying to cheer you up, Mal." Eris says innocently.

I don't believe that for a second.

"Fine, but play nice." Set commands her.

"I can do that."

We all drink and recount the days when we were all together. True to her word, Eris played nice and did not bring up Olive or try to make a move on me all night. Sometime before dawn, Set passes out, leaving Eris and me alone. We sit in silence, looking up at the sky for a long while before she speaks.

"I really am sorry about your female."

"Eris, I do not want to talk about her."

"I know. I just hate that you are here, sad, and she is in the human realm with her mortal love, happy."

"How do you even know any of that?" I turn to look at her.

"Do not be mad, but I maybe definitely spied on her."

"Damn it, Eris."

"I could not help it, Mal."

"Is she okay?" I ask.

"Oh yes, he is taking great care of her if you know what I mean."

Unfortunately, I do, and I feel sick to my stomach.

"She is at his house, if you want to go see for yourself."

"No. I know she needs to figure things out for herself. We will be together in the end." I do not know if I am trying to convince Eris or myself of this.

"Come on, just to make sure she is okay."

I do want to see Olive. Maybe just a quick check. She does not even have to know I was there.

"Fine, but I am just checking on her and coming back, Eris."

"Absolutely, just a quick peek."

We get to Mark's house and end up in his room. I see Olive. She is curled up to Mark's chest, wrapped in his arms, and obviously naked. I feel sick. It would be one thing if she chose both of us, but it feels like she is choosing him only, and my heart is breaking. This was a bad idea. Olive must sense us there because she opens her eyes and sits up, catching the blanket right before it reveals her naked breast. I cannot do this any longer.

"Malsumis?" Olive whispers.

"Oh, how delicious. The goddess of dreams reduced to mortal pleasures. Did you really think that Mal would not find out?" Eris spits.

"Olive, who…" Marks starts, then feels the weight of our presence and stops. He instinctively pulls Olive closer to him to protect her. Not that he could, but at least his effort is valiant.

"Are you choosing him, Olive?" I say, stepping forward, my voice low and rough.

"Malsumis, I…" She starts, but a sob stops her from finishing before Eris interrupts.

"This is too perfect. The goddess torn between her god and her mortal. How will you choose, dreamer? Which heart will you break?" Eris taunts, voice sounding like splintering glass.

I step back, fist clenched at my sides. My soul feels as though it is unraveling. I am standing here, not as a god but as a male who gave away his heart and is now feeling it shatter.

"Malsumis, wait…" Olive calls, but I do not stay to listen.

Chapter 21: Olive

He's gone. He didn't even let me explain; he just left.

"Oh, poor dreamer. Don't you worry, I will comfort Mal." Eris antagonizes before she disappears.

I look at Mark, my eyes filling with tears. He gathers me in his arms and pulls me close.

"We will get him back. We will explain things. It will work out, Olive." He said, continuing to hold me as I cry.

"I'm sorry. I can't imagine how this makes you feel. I love you so much, but I love him too."

"I understand, and I am willing to do whatever it takes to make this work. We will figure this out."

"I need to go after him." I jump out of bed to find clothes to slide on.

"Do you even know where he went?"

"I think I have an idea. I have to try something, you know."

"Let me come with you," Mark says, getting up to get dressed himself.

"I can't, not where I have to go. If I can't find him, I will come back, and we will come up with a new plan."

"You can't or you won't?"

"Both. I don't know what to expect when I get there, and I will not put you in harm's way." I walk up to him and hold his face in my hands, "I can't lose you." I kiss him softly and then go to find Malsumis.

I appear in Set's rooms and find them empty. I make my way through the halls to the gardens, and I know Malsumis likes it there. I get to the middle of the gardens and find a very passed out Set. I rush over to him and try to wake him up.

"Come on, Set, wake up. I need you!"

"Hmmm. You need me? I have been waiting to hear that." He mumbles.

"Oh, gods, Set! I need to find Malsumis."

"Boo, you tease. He is here with Eris and me."

"No, he isn't. They came to me in the human realm. He saw me with Mark, left upset, and Eris followed. I need to find him."

"Shit, I should have known Eris was up to something last

night. It felt like old times, and I guess I wanted to hang on to that. Fuck."

"I know you love her, but she is up to something with Malsumis."

"Love her? Olive, there is no love there. It has only ever been friendship, and lately it has only been physical. I assure you, I do not love her."

"Then you won't mind helping me get her away from him."

"Not at all. Does this mean you want him back?"

"Yes. I have to talk with him, but I want him."

"It's about time. What about the mortal?"

"Well…I love him too."

"Oh, I see. Care to add a third?" Set says with a wink. I look at him with an arched brow.

"Do you have any idea where he might be?"

"Yes, but let me check things out. I will find you and give you an update."

"Thank you, Set." I hug him.

"I will do anything you want if you keep touching me," he chuckles. I roll my eyes and head back to Mark's.

I appear in the bedroom, and the sunlight is coming through the windows. I was gone most of the night and morning. Mark is not in here, so I walk out to the living room and find him on the couch, asleep. I walk over to him and admire how beautiful he is. I place my hand on his head, sending him soothing dreams. I have someone I need to deal with before he wakes.

I take one more look at Mark and go into my dream realm. I see her curled into herself in the darkness.

"Hello, Grandmother."

"Olive, please let me go. I'm sorry. I will do anything."

"I don't want anything from you anymore. All I ever wanted was love, and all you ever did was push me away and put me down. I have found my family. I realize I don't need this revenge. I don't need you at all. You are nothing to me, just like I was to you."

"Please let me go." She whispers.

"Go back to your existence. That is what it is. You're not living; you just exist to be hateful and evil. I release you. Goodbye." She vanishes, and I take a deep breath.

I think of Malsumis trying to find him within the realm, but every time I get close, there is some kind of haze, and I can't quite reach him. I try again with the same results. I haven't had this problem before. I will mention it to Set and see what he thinks of it.

When I get back to Mark's, I am shocked to find Set there…with Mark…playing video games.

Chapter 22: Mark

She left just like he did. Is that how this is going to be? Something happens, and she just leaves? We are definitely going to talk about this. I don't want to be left behind all the time.

I sit on the couch and wait for hours. The sun starts to come up, and she still isn't back. I begin to doze off. At first, my sleep is restless, but I soon fall into a soothing sleep with dreams of Olive and me watching movies together, laughing, and kissing. I wake to sounds in the kitchen. Thinking it is Olive, I go in, but it is not Olive that I find rummaging through my fridge.

"Excuse me, what in the hell are you doing in my house?" The man, or god, who stands before me just smiles a smile that threatens to make me melt immediately.

"Hello, mortal. I am Set."

"Set. Of course you are. What are you doing in my kitchen, Set?"

"Currently, looking for wine."

"I'm fresh out. Had I known you were stopping by, I would have bought some," I quip, leaning against the counter, acting as nonchalant as I can, even though I am freaking out inside. " I assume you're here for Olive?"

"Oh yes, the lovely Olive."

"Watch it."

"Feisty mortal. I like it."

"My name is Mark, and she isn't back yet. You are welcome to wait for her in the living room, though."

We sit in silence for some very awkward moments before I try to start a conversation.

"So, do you want to watch TV or play some video games?"

"I have never played video games." Set says, "Show me how."

Set comes over and sinks into the couch beside me, tilting his head slightly, studying my character on the screen. I hold out the other controller to him, and he takes it in his massive hand. I quickly show him what the buttons do. Within minutes, I am playing games with a god, and oddly, that's not shocking to me. Soon, Set is totally immersed and leaning forward. When his character flies off the map, I laugh.

"Unfair!" He booms, though his eyes gleam with mischief. "This tiny box cheats!"

By the time Olive arrives back, we are shoulder to shoulder, locked in a heated match. I double over in laughter as Set shouts at the screen.

"I see you have met Set," Olive says as she comes to sit beside me.

"I have." I lean into her and whisper, "You and I need to talk later." She looks at me with tears in her eyes, and I almost fold, but Set interrupts the moment.

"I found Mal."

"Where is he? Is he okay?" Olive anxiously asks.

"He is in his realm of chaos that he created long ago. No, it is not okay. Eris has woven some kind of spell. She was not there when I was, but I expect she will be checking in on him."

"I tried to reach him from my dream realm, and there was some kind of haze blocking me from him. That must be Eris's work."

"How do we help him?" I interject. They both look at me. "I am going to help. Somehow. I want to help."

"I like your courage mor…Mark. I do not think that you know the dangers that you might find dealing with Eris or even Mal in this state."

"If Mark wants to help, then that is what will happen." Olive declares, looking at me proudly.

"Well, okay. With that settled, welcome to the club, Mark." Set chuckles and claps me on the back.

"I'm going to go to his realm and try to get through to him," Olive states.

"If anyone can get him back, it is you. It may take more than one visit, but between us, we will figure this out. You go, and I will stay here with Mark. I have a score to settle with this little box."

"I can go with you." I turn and take Olive's face in my hands.

"Not this time. I know what he is capable of when he isn't himself, and I can't risk you. I promise you will be at my side whenever you can be."

"I want to be a part of this as much as I can. I want this to work out for us." I kiss her softly.

"Either stop the lovey dovey or come over and share the love," Set butts in, wagging his eyebrows.

Olive rolls her eyes and throws a pillow from the couch at him. His laughter booms in the room. Olive turns back to me and kisses me again.

"I will be back as fast as I can."

"I love you. Please be careful."

"I will. I love you so much," with one last kiss, she leaves.

Chapter 23: Malsumis

I cannot remember the last time I was in this realm, my realm, but I did not know where else to go to be alone. I knew Olive was with Mark, but when I saw her in bed with him, I had to leave. It felt like she was choosing him.

"Olive is looking for you." Set's deep voice interrupts my thoughts.

"She has the mortal now."

"She still loves you, Mal."

"She has an odd way of showing it."

"You knew where she was, and you still went. What did you expect to find, Mal? You knew."

"Do you need anything else, Set?"

"Come back with me. Come see her."

"Leave, Set."

"Mal, something strange is going on here. Eris is not your friend anymore. Come back with me."

"Leave, Set. Now."

"Fine, but I will be back. I will not let you go, my friend." He vows, and then he is gone.

I should have let her speak. What if I am wrong? What if she wants me too? I need to go back.

"Are you okay?" Eris's concerned voice comes from behind me.

"What do you want?"

"I want to check on you, Mal."

"You are the reason this happened! I should have never listened to you."

"Come on, Mal, I was trying to help."

"No, you were trying to pull me away from Olive, and that is not going to happen."

"You are here, are you not?"

I narrow my eyes at her and try to leave. It does not work. I look around and try again. It is as though I am stuck. I look at Eris, who is smiling smugly.

"WHAT HAVE YOU DONE?" I thunder as I stalk over to Eris.

"Did you really think that you would come back and deny me? I always get what I want, and I want you, Mal. I just have to wait for you to see you want me too." Before I reach her, she is gone.

I am trapped. I thought this would never happen again. How could I be so stupid? I underestimated Eris. Fuck. I try to calm myself and call out to Set. Nothing. I take a deep breath and try to reach out to my Olive. I get a splitting pain in my head. I start to panic. I try Set again. Still nothing, but no pain either. I try Olive, and the pain returns. What has Eris done to me?

"Malsumis?" Olive's soft voice breaks the silence. I take a shaky breath.

"My Olive."

I feel her arms wrap around me from behind. I have missed her touch. How could I ever think I could be without her?

"I wanted to explain things to you, but I couldn't find you. Then, when you came to Mark's, you left again. I am so sorry you saw that before I could explain how I feel. I love you, Malsumis. I want to be with you, too. If you will have me."

"Oh my Olive, my mate, we will find a way to make this work for us." I turn to look at her, and when I do, I am overcome with anger. I push her away quickly and close my eyes. The anger subsides. "Get away from me!"

"Wh…what is going on? Malsumis? Are you okay?"

"Stay away from me! Something is wrong. When I looked at you, I wanted to hurt you. Eris has done something to me. She has trapped me here and is trying to turn me against you." "I am going to kill her." Olive's voice is deadly.

"Don't, Olive. I am not worth risking yourself over."

"Malsumis, you are everything. You are more than worth the risk. We are going to figure out how to get you out of here and lift this spell or whatever it is."

"Who is we?"

"Set, Mark, and me."

"Mark will help to save me?"

"Yes, he is adamant that we will figure out a way for all of us to work. Keep your eyes closed." She walks to me and reaches up to my face. I bend down to her, and she claims a kiss from my lips. "I love you. We will be back for you. Fight this and know we are fighting too."

"I love you, my heart, my Olive. I will fight." She kisses me again and then leaves me to the silence of my own realm.

Chapter 24: Olive

I'm vibrating with anger when I get back to Mark's. How dare she trap him! How dare she try to take what is mine! I know I was confused at first, but I'm not anymore. I was kidding myself thinking that I could be without Malsumis.

As I enter the room, Set and Mark immediately stand, feeling the rage rolling off of me.

"That bitch is going to pay for what she is doing to him."

"What happened while you were there?" Mark asks.

"She has him trapped there and has him under a spell. If he looks at me, he tries to attack. As long as he doesn't see me, he is normal. We have to free him. Set, please tell me you have some idea of how to break this spell."

"I can speak with my father about this. He will not be happy at all, and I am sure will allow us to do what is necessary to free Mal. Ultimately, Mal has to be strong enough to fight this. Keep visiting him and encouraging him."

"Do you think his family would help?" Mark suggests. I turn and look at Set.

"I do not believe it will hurt to ask. I do not expect them to, but we need all the help we can get."

"I will go with Olive and speak with Malsumis's family." Mark declares.

"I will go speak with Father now and then check on Mal," Set says with a nod, then is gone. I turn to Mark.

"You need rest."

"Don't do that. Don't put me on the sidelines, and don't just leave like you did before. I know I am different from you now, but I can still be there with and for you."

"I'm sorry. I didn't mean to make you feel less. I can't lose you, and I am so scared."

"I get it, and at some point we will have to face the fact that either I am going to age or be injured and die, but not right now, okay?"

"Or we figure out a way to make you immortal…" I offer.

"There's that too. For now, let's focus on saving Malsumis."

Mark and I enter the realm of the Great Spirit, and it is like nothing I have ever seen before. Before us is a giant tree with branches that stretch far over fields on one side and a vibrant blue river on the other. I can only assume that this is the Tree of Life. Behind us are vast hills and valleys of green speckled with color here and there. Suddenly, the air is heavy; it reminds me of when Malsumis would get upset. Malsumis's father appears in front of us, standing tall and strong, like the tree behind him. His long, raven black hair is braided with feathers and beads and flows down his tan skin. He is wearing tanned hides and a tunic with intricate beadwork. I look into his light amber eyes.

"You come seeking aid?"

"We are here seeking help for Malsumis. Eris has him trapped in his realm. She has a spell woven in his mind." I bow my head in respect.

"No. Just as when he sought help with you, Olive, what is set into motion must run its course. Malsumis must walk this path without my aid."

"So you would let your son be destroyed? Let him be manipulated?" Mark spits, his hands clenched in fists at his sides.

"I am not cruel. I am balance. To intervene would tip the scales and that I cannot do."

My throat burns with a scream I can't release. My eyes are filling with unshed tears, but I know the truth. His words are final. The Great Spirit turns from us, and the realm begins to fade. He is kicking us out. I take us back to Mark's living room.

We both collapse onto the couch in silence, not sure how to process what just happened. I look around and realize how late it is. Mark still has an entire life to live, and I have not made sure he was taken care of. I look over at him. He looks tired, and I know he has to be hungry.

"You need to eat and rest. You still have a life beyond us."

"You are my life, Olive. I am going to use vacation time and say I am helping you move back. I told you I am going to be at your side."

"Well, you are my life too, and I want to make sure that you are taken care of. So, you are going to eat and rest."

"Yes, my goddess," he smirks.

"Oh, I like that," I tease back, sliding over to straddle him. "Now you sit here while I make you some food."

"Suddenly, I'm not so hungry," he mumbles as he begins kissing down my neck.

"Nope! I'm going to take care of you." I exclaim and jump up.

"Technically, you would be," he says, laughing.

I go to the kitchen and rummage through his fridge. He usually has more food than this in his house. I knew he struggled while I was gone, but I guess I didn't realize it affected even the way he ate. There is turkey and cheese, so I throw together a quick sandwich. When I go back over to the couch, Mark is asleep. I put his sandwich in the refrigerator and write a quick note letting him know I am going to visit Malsumis. I put the note on the coffee table beside him, then cover him up with a blanket and send soothing dreams through to him before I leave.

I return to Malsumis's realm and am stunned by the beauty that surrounds me. I saw it before, but this time I really take it in. The sun is hanging low on the horizon. It's light spilling streaks of gold and fire across the sky. I am standing in a field of tall grasses that are swaying in a strong breeze that wasn't here last time. The air is heavy and warm, tinged with an earthy scent. Malsumis's scent. Then I see him not too far ahead with his back to me. Time feels suspended for a moment as I watch him. His long hair flows with the wind. His shoulders are slumped like the weight of everything is just too much. I walk up behind him and wrap my arms around him. He tenses until he hears my voice.

"I'm here, my Love." He relaxes in my arms and places a hand over mine.

"I cannot take this. I am not strong enough."

"You're strong enough. We are working on breaking this spell. Just hang on. Please don't give up, Malsumis." He turns around and holds me close.

"I promise, my Olive, I will not surrender." With his eyes still closed, he leans down, and I capture his lips in a kiss. It starts soft and quickly turns into something desperate, leaving us both out of breath.

"I love you," I breathe into his lips before his mouth crashes into mine again.

He lifts me, and I wrap my legs around him. Every movement is grounded in the raw need for one another. He holds up with his hands on my ass as he kneels to his knees, so I am straddling him. Thank gods I am wearing a dress. I kiss my way down his neck as he begins to free himself. Then we hear her.

"Oh my, what a show I have stumbled upon. Don't stop on my account." Eris croons sarcastically, breaking our moment, causing Malsumis to open his eyes.

He looks at me, and I see the change. He throws me to the ground, and his hand goes to my throat. I begin to panic. This isn't him. I have to get through to him.

"Malsumis, please." I get out.

"Oh, darling Dreamer, your pleas won't work. Go ahead, Mal."

"Olive…leave…now…" Malsumis says through clenched teeth as he fights back.

"I love you, Malsumis." I breathe, and then I disappear.

✳✳✳

I get back to Mark's to find him still sleeping on the couch. I must have only been gone a few hours. I feel defeated. Malsumis needs my help, and I don't know what to do. I feel so lost.

"Hey, you," Mark says sleepily.

"I'm sorry. I didn't mean to wake you."

"Oh no, you didn't. I woke up a little bit ago and saw your note. I tried to wait up for you, but I dozed back off."

"Let's go to bed. I don't know if I can sleep, but I definitely need to be close to you."

"It went that good, huh?"

"I just feel like I am failing him."

"Hey, you are not failing him." Mark takes my face in his hands. "He knows that we are looking for a way to free him from the spell. You are doing everything you can. Now, it's time for me to take care of you. You look exhausted. It's time to rest."

"You know, technically, I don't need sleep."

"I know, but humor me. Please, baby."

"How am I supposed to resist pet names?" I laugh softly. "I'm sure you're ready to have your bed back to yourself. I mean, I have to go back to my house at some point." His face becomes serious.

"Why would you think that? This is our house. This is our bed. Unless you would rather stay at the other house, I thought we would wait for Malsumis to make that decision. Just know where you go, I go. You are stuck with me, Babygirl.”

“I guess I am okay with being stuck with you,” I tease.

“Oh, you better run!” He teases back and chases me towards the bedroom. Just as he reaches me, there is a loud knock at the front door. We look at each other and head to the door. “Stay behind me.” He protectively stands in front of me while he opens the door.

Standing in front of us is an almost exact copy of Malsumis. Almost. His eyes are wrong; they are brown, not black. His face a little more rounded. This is not my Mal.

“Who are you?” I question from behind Mark.

“I am Gluskap. Malsumis’s brother.”

Chapter 25: Malsumis

Olive is gone, and I turn my rage to Eris. I stalk toward her, and she stumbles backward, eyes wide, as I do. I go to grab her.

"STOP!" She commands me. I freeze. My feet will not go any further.

"What have you done?" I snarl.

"What I needed to do to protect myself," she explains as she straightens her dress. "I can't have you turning on me now, can I?"

"Eris, release me," I order her.

"You will be released from this when I leave," she says, coming closer and putting her hand on my face. I turn away. "Oh, Mal, stop fighting this. We can be great together again." She tries to kiss me. I panic, then get angry, and break through her command, pushing her away.

"Do not touch me, Eris! What we had is finished. It was finished long before I was trapped in the human realm. Undo this spell!"

"No! I do not accept this! I will not accept this! You are mine! Olive is already back with her mortal, and you are still pining for her!" She yells.

"You need not worry yourself with Olive and my arrangement. Let. Me. Go."

"No." Crossing her arms like a petulant child. "I will destroy her before she has you." Then Eris is gone.

Panic flows through my body. I am stuck here, and Eris just threatened Olive. I need to warn her. I am blocked from calling her directly, and that would be what Eris would want anyway. I call out to Set. In a matter of seconds, he is beside me.

"I am sorry I have not been back, Mal. We are working on a way to free you. Zeus is being…uncooperative." Set starts.

"Set, stop. Eris has threatened Olive's life. I need you to warn and help protect her."

"Shit. I will do this. Mal, you have to fight Eris. You may be the only one who can."

"I am trying. Please just protect Olive…and Mark," Set looks at me inquisitively. "He means something to Olive, so try to keep him alive."

"I will keep them safe."

I nod at him in acknowledgement and thanks, then he is gone. I am alone once more, what I wouldn't do to be in Olive's arms right now. I have to hold on to the fact that she still loves me. That she wants me. I feel stronger thinking of her and our love. I will keep fighting for us.

"She does not want you. What can you offer her? So easily tricked. Pathetic."

I turn to see who is whispering and see no one. This is one of Eris's mind games. I sit and try to focus on Olive and happier memories of us.

"She has her mortal. She no longer loves you. She no longer needs you."

All lies. None of this is true. I keep reminding myself. Over and over again, I say to myself, "Lies all lies."

"She is with her mortal lover now. She has forgotten you here." More lies.

"You were never good enough for her. You are weak. She will always choose him over you." Not true. Right?

"Oh, Mal, you will see that I am the only one who truly loves you for you."

I cover my ears, but it does nothing to keep the whispers from reaching me. The assault continues as I try to stay focused on my Olive.

Chapter 26: Olive

"We have already been to see your father, and he denied us. What are you doing here?" Mark questions impatiently.

"I am not here on behalf of my father. I have come to help Malsumis."

"Come in. Let's talk." I usher Gluskap in toward the living room.

"Are you sure we can trust him?" Mark whispers in my ear.

"I hope so. Malsumis needs us." I whisper back as we all take a seat.

"How do we save Malsumis?" Mark asks plainly and fearlessly.

"I do not know exactly, but I do have an idea. Eris is all about causing strife and leaving her victims hopeless. We need to give him hope and show him how loved he is to help him fight her."

"No offense, but you aren't close with your brother. The only way I knew of you was from Set and your father." I counter.

"You are right. We are not close. Now. We once were, though. I do love my brother."

"What happened between the two of you?" I ask.

"As I mentioned, when we were young, we were close. We were both given the same powers by our father to help humans, and that is what we did. We taught them to hunt, grow food, and build shelter, but Malsumis never got the love and praise he deserved from the humans or our father. I saw that and tried to help him, but he thought I pitied him, and it did not go over well. He began to act out. It began with small things, such as putting stingers on bees and thorns on roses. Pranks on humans that caused more tension between them and Malsumis.

Soon, his anger grew, turning more destructive. Earthquakes, storms, fires. I loved him through it all and hoped it all was a phase, but after many years, I had to accept that he was chaos. He went down a path I couldn't follow. On our last day together, we argued, and he gave me this back," he holds out an ancient necklace. "I had given this to him when we were young. I held on to it all these years in hopes of us finding our way back to each other."

"Now is your chance," Mark says.

"He will not want to see me."

"You have to try. You have to help remind him that he is loved. You defied your father to be here. What better way to show Malsumis you love him?" I say.

"WHAT THE FUCK IS HE DOING HERE?" Set booms, interrupting.

"Whoa, Set, calm down! He is here to help Malsumis fight Eris." I jump between Set and Gluskap.

"What, so he can abandon him again? That is what you and your father are good at." Set accuses from around me. Mark joins me in trying to calm Set.

"I was skeptical at first, too, man, but he seems like he genuinely wants to help his brother. Hell, he is here against his father's wishes." Mark says calmly.

"Fine. If you hurt him again, I will be coming for you." Set promises, Gluskap.

"I love my brother. I regret how things happened all those years ago. I will not let that happen again."

"So what is the plan?" Mark says, breaking the tension and sliding an arm around my waist.

"First, Mal has sent me here because Eris has threatened Olive. I intend on helping protect you." Set informs us. Mark tenses beside me, tightening his arm around me.

"I just got Olive back. I am not losing her again. How do we take Eris down?"

"It will come down to a battle between Malsumis and Eris, I am afraid. Father has seen this." Gluskap speaks up.

"Did your father see the outcome of this battle?" Mark asks.

"No."

"Convenient." Set remarks. I give Set a look.

"Okay, so back to how to free Malsumis. So we all just go to him and remind him we love him? Do we go together?" I ask Gluskap.

"I believe if we go together and show a united front, it will have the greatest effect. It will also draw Eris out, forcing her into a battle unprepared," he answers.

"Okay, so let's go," Mark says eagerly.

"We all need to be rested and at full strength. We can stay here for a few hours and then go, just in case Mal needs to pull from us." Set suggests.

"Gluskap, why don't you take the guest room, and Set, you take the living room in case we need anything from our room," I order.

"Is that an invite? Because I am in." Set flirts. I just roll my eyes and follow Mark to our room.

Once the door to our room closes, Mark grabs me and pulls me close, kissing me deeply. His tongue slides against mine with urgency and need. We are both breathless when we part.

"I can't lose you again, baby."

"You won't. You're stuck with me."

"Let's get some rest so we can help Mal."

"Mark, I don't want you to go. I'm scared something will happen."

"I can't stay here. He needs everyone he can get on his side. If we are going to try to work out some kind of relationship, I need him to know I forgive him, too."

"I love you so much. Please stay back and don't be upset if I send you back if this gets too crazy."

"Okay, my girl, I promise. I love you," he says, kissing me on the forehead, and we climb into bed.

Mark is asleep within minutes. His soft snores lull me into a rest as well. I try reaching out to Malsumis. There is still a haze where he should be. It is like a web when I get close to it. I try to fight my way through when I hear her voice.

"Ah, the dreamer. Don't worry, I am taking good care of him. He has forgotten all about you."

"I highly doubt that. We are mates, that is not something you just forget, Eris. Let him go."

"Well, his kisses suggest otherwise, Dreamer," she giggles. Jealousy flares through me, then dread. What is she forcing him to do?

"Keep your fucking hands off of him!" I yell.

"Oh, but he loves my hands…and my lips…among other things…" she cackles.

"I will end you, Eris," I snarl.

"Olive?" I hear Malsumis's voice break through.

"Malsumis, I love you. Remember how much I love you." I answer back.

"Yes, you love him enough to deny him over and over and then take a mortal lover." Eris spits.

"You know nothing about us. Stay away from my mate!" I scream at her.

All I hear is her laugh as she pushes me away from Malsumis. I almost fight back to stay close to him, but I remember that I need to save my strength for him later, so I let her think she is in control…for now.

Chapter 27: Malsumis

I have been listening to Eris's whispers for what feels like ages. I am trying to block them out, but some of them are beginning to creep in. What if Olive is better off without me? Maybe I am a pathetic waste. No one but Set and Eris has ever really stood by me. Not even my own family loves me.

Suddenly, I hear her. Olive. My Olive. She is trying to reach me. She has not forgotten me at all. Lies. Eris only spews lies. I call out for Olive, and she reminds me of how much she loves me.
I hear her arguing with Eris over me. My girl is fearless. Everything comes back to me now. Olive does love me. She does want to be with me. Eris has trapped me. I know that I have to fight her to be free, but am I strong enough? At least Olive will have Mark if I am not.

I settle back in for the continued assault, but it does not come. Apparently, Eris is giving me a moment of peace. I use it to lie back in the grass and rest in the silence.

"Wake up, Malsumis," I hear Olive's voice. It is a little off, but I am so happy she is back that I pay no attention to it.

"My Olive, I am so glad you are back."

"Open your eyes." I am nervous to do so, but I do as she asks. When I see her, I feel no anger; I feel fine. "Olive, I must be unraveling the spell because I can look at you again!" I go to her and pull her into my arms. I notice that her eyes are not quite as bright as they usually are, and her hair is not as lustrous. I am just glad to hold her again. Still, my mind screams this is wrong.

"Oh, how I have missed you," she whispers in my ear, sending shivers through my body. I cannot stop myself from claiming her lips with mine. Her kiss is untamed and aggressive. I give in even though my mind still screams to stop.

Her hands roam over my body with wicked intention. I match her eagerness with my own. Our touches turning into more. We hurriedly undress while trying not to break our kiss. She pushes me to the ground and climbs onto me, and my hands go to her hips and guide her rhythm. Her moans grow louder, and her pace becomes more erratic. When she finds her release, I have not, but I do not care; I just want to be with my Olive. I sit up, pulling her close and begin kissing down the column of her neck, pausing to breathe her in. Alarms go off in my head. Her smell is wrong. This is not the calm vanilla and lavender of my Olive. This is the smell of incense and spice. This is Eris.

I pull back and look up. I am looking into Eris's deep green eyes. As if a spell has been broken, I push her off of me, jump up and back away quickly, shaking my head.

"Boo. I was hoping it would take you longer to figure it out," she pouts.

"How could you do this, Eris?"

"I got tired of waiting," she shrugs nonchalantly.

I drop to my knees, head in my hands. How could I be so stupid? How am I going to tell Olive?

"Oh gods, Mal, it was nothing we have not done before. It is not that big of a deal."

"You tricked me into doing those things. I would have never touched you if I knew you were not Olive."

"This is boring. I will be back when you're less pathetic," she huffs and then is gone.

I vomit.

Chapter 28: Mark

I wake hours later next to Olive. I look over at her. She is ethereal. Her hair cascades on the pillow in soft, pale waves. Lying like this in the moonlight, her skin has an otherworldly glow. She looks over at me, feeling my gaze on her. Those eyes. Crystalline and impossibly blue. They are calm yet endless, as if they could see far beyond the veil of the ordinary world. I chuckle to myself because, technically, they can.

"What's so funny?" She asks.

"Just wondering what I did to get so lucky to land you."

She smiles and leans in to kiss me. A knock on the door breaks the moment.

"I will be glad when this is over; it has been far too long since I have been in you."

"MARK!" She giggles and swats me on the chest. "You're so dirty!"

"You like it."

"I didn't say I didn't," she laughs.

We get up and get ready. We walk out to the most uncomfortable silence in the history of silences. "There you two are. I thought I was going to have to come in and join you." Set jokes.

"You couldn't handle us, Set," I tease with a wink at him. He smirks back.

"If you two are finished flirting, I would like to go get Malsumis now, please and thank you," Olive interrupts.

"Don't be jealous, babe," I kiss her head, and she just rolls her eyes. I lean down to her ear, "If you keep rolling your eyes at me, I'm going to spank you for that later." Her eyes go wide.

"Promise?" She smirks.

"If you all are ready, we should go," Gluskap clears his throat.

I must admit that I am nervous, but I know this is the right thing to do. I grab Olive's hand and kiss it. She turns and smiles up at me. I love her so much. I never thought I could feel like this about someone. She may be Malsumis's mate in the god realm, but here in the human world, she was an inevitability that I couldn't avoid.
Not that I would ever want to. She is perfect.

"I love you, Baby."

"I love you more than you will ever know, Babe."

"Oh, a pet name! I like it," I tease. She just smiles and leans up for a kiss, which I happily give her.

"Keep holding on to my hand, and I will take you with me to Malsumis's realm. Ready?"
"As I will ever be."

"Let's go get our boy," Set says from beside us.

I close my eyes, and when I open them, I am in Malsumis's realm. It is, honestly, well, gorgeous. The sky is painted in reds, oranges, and golds. There are fields of tall grasses swaying in a gentle breeze. It is eerily calm for a god of chaos…the calm before the storm.

I see Malsumis then. We all do. He is kneeling in the tall grasses with his head down. Defeated. This isn't good.

"Malsumis?" Olive says quietly.

"No more tricks, Eris. Please." Malsumis begs, heartbreakingly.

"It's not Eris. It's Olive, my Love." She walks over to him and wraps her arms around the top of his shoulders, and whispers something only he can hear. His shoulders begin to shake softly as he begins to cry. He pulls her around to the front of him and holds her tightly, burying his face in the crook of her neck.

After a moment, he stands and puts her behind him, still holding her hand. He opens his eyes. At first, there is a look of shock as he takes in his brother and me.

"Olive, Set, what is this? What has taken you so long?" he asks.

"Mal, it has only been two days since I was last here," Set explains.

"Two days? It has felt like months…" Malsumis says sadly.

"Gluskap believes your best chance at defeating Eris is to have us all here to remind you how much we all love and care about you. I will help you fight her." Set explains.

"No. I must do this myself. I will not have you or Olive in harm's way," he says, looking at me next. "Since when did you start caring, Mark? Before or after you punched me in the face?"

"First of all, you deserved that. Second, I have had time to reflect. We both love Olive, and I am willing to do anything to make her happy. If she forgives you, then I forgive you. I don't wish anything like this on anyone. I want you to be free so we can work on things between us." I tell him. He looks surprised but nods in appreciation and moves on to his brother.

"Hello, Brother. The last time I saw you, I was told you could no longer be around me. What brings you here?" Malsumis's anger is palpable. There is something else there, though. Hurt?

"I was wrong, Malsumis. You needed me, and I turned my back on you. I will always carry that. I do not expect forgiveness, but I love you, brother. I always have. I never stopped." Gluskap walks to Malsumis and holds out the necklace he has carried all these years.

Malsumis takes the necklace from his brother. He holds it, turning it over in his hand, staring at it, like he doesn't believe what he is seeing. With tears in his eyes, he looks at his brother.

"You kept this," he says, almost at a whisper.

"It never left my possession, brother."

They look at each other for a moment, not knowing what to say or do. Then Malsumis embraces his brother. Gluskap relaxes in his brother's arms, like some of the weight of the guilt he has been carrying has been lifted. Mal's shoulders shake slightly as if he is crying. Then it all makes sense to me. Malsumis has been chasing love and acceptance his whole life. No wonder that when Eris acted as she cared, he trusted her again.

"Oh, how sweet," someone coos from behind Set and me.

"Eris, lift this spell you have woven over Mal. This is neither funny nor cute. This is enough." Set says sternly, turning to her.

"Do be jealous, Set. We can all be together again. I am doing this for us, darling."

"Enough, Eris. There is no us anymore. We all have moved on from those days." Malsumis comes back at her.

"NO, YOU MOVED ON, MAL! I AM STILL HERE WAITING FOR YOU!" Eris screams. She unfurls her power, which looks like deep crimson strands of shadow, and throws it toward Malsumis. He looks shocked but is able to get himself and Olive out of the way.

"Eris, do not do this. Undo this spell and walk away. Please." Malsumis tries to talk to her. She is beyond such, and she sends another wave at him, narrowly missing him.

Gluskap makes his way to Olive and pulls her over to us out of the way of Eris's wrath. I wrap her in my arms. I know in the scheme of things I can't really do anything to protect her, but I would die trying.

"Mark, protect Olive," Malsumis calls to me before turning back to Eris.

The air is thick and seems to pulse with Eris's magic. Thick, suffocating. She circles Malsumis like a serpent, her sharp smile making me sick to my stomach. She reaches up and trails her fingers along his jaw. Olive stills in my arms and goes to pull away. I hold her back.

"He has this baby. Let him do this." I say quietly into her ear.

Then I hear Eris's whispers to Malsumis.

"You are mine," she hisses, "You belong to me. You will destroy with me again. You will love me."

For a heartbeat, he seems to be snagged under her spell even more, and Olive sags in my arms, defeated. We all hold our breath.
Just when I think all is lost, something within him shifts.

Chapter 29: Malsumis

My body feels like a prisoner, and my mind is beginning to cloud over. No. NO. I will not let this happen. Everything I love is here with me…plus Mark. They all care and love me. I will be strong for them. For myself. I remember Olive's lips on mine, her voice, her laughter. My brothers embrace. Set's constant friendship. Mark caring enough to show up for me after everything.

The fog burned away.

My eyes snap open. Eris's enchantments no longer hold me. The bindings of her spell cannot hold my chaos any longer. Cracks split them like lightning across the sky.

"No," Eris whispers, her smile faltering. She pulls harder at her bindings. Desperate, her magic screams through the air. "YOU ARE NOTHING WITHOUT ME!" She bellows.

I straighten to my full height and release my full power. Her chains shatter in a storm of sparks, exploding outward. I take the last of her power clinging to me and tear it apart with a roar that shakes the ground we stand on. A cyclone of raw energy erupted from my hands toward Eris, causing her to stagger backward.

"You have never and will never own me!" I thundered at her.

I see the others standing back, just as I asked, watching this unfold. I want to keep them safely away from the battle that is about to ensue, so I create a storm encompassing Eris and me. I hear Olive call for me, but I cannot go to her yet. I am going to deal with Eris once and for all.

I stand in the center of the storm I have created, letting my powers radiate from me in waves of black that warp the air itself. Eris staggers back but recovers quickly. Her smile snaps back into place, although there is a hint of fear in her eyes. With a snarl, she flings her hands forward, and ribbons of crimson shadow, twisting into spears, fly toward me. I raise my arms, and the storm responds by sending the blades curving around me. The storm swallows and shatters them into sparks as they pass by me.

"You believe love makes you strong?" she spits, her voice cracking with fury. "It will break you. It will always break you!"

Her words lash out like whips, dripping with venom meant to pierce my mind, but they fall flat. I stride forward to her, my eyes never leaving hers.

"Love does not bind me," I tell her, "It frees me."

She shrieks, summoning a vortex of darkness and discord. Her form twists into a monstrous creature with wings of smoke and claws of glass. She hurls herself upon me like a tidal wave. I do not flinch. I raise both hands and gather all of my chaos into an overwhelming surge. My storm meets hers in a clash of shadows that block out the heavens. For many moments, neither of us yields. The world trembles beneath us. Then I let go, not of my power, but of the restraint I have carried since I was first trapped in the human realm. I release all the built up anger I have held onto for many centuries. Chaos in its truest form, unmastered, unbroken, surges through me.

Her darkness shatters. Her screams tear through the air as her body is hurled back, crashing into the fractured ground. She rises defiant, bleeding, warped by rage.

"You will regret this, Malsumis," she hisses, summoning the last of her power.

"No, Eris. You will."

My power gathers once more and descends upon her. The ground splits wide beneath us, Eris stands in the rubble, her body cracked and bleeding.

"You cannot kill me!" she shrieks, "I am discord. I can control you."

I do not answer, I only walk to her steadily and unshaken. She hurls everything she can at me, but none of it touches me now. Every weapon melts into the storm around us. I raise my hand and concentrate my power into a single point. Chaos itself is bowing to me, not as a master, not as a prisoner, but in acceptance of my true nature. Her eyes widen, and panic replaces the mask of anger. She scrambles backward and claws at the air to get her power to listen to her, but it fails.

"No. NO! You are mine! You will always be mine!"

"I was never yours." With those words, her fate was sealed, my voice carrying her doom.

The storm falls upon her with crimson and black shadows intertwined, crushing her scream into silence. Her body convulsed, her form splinters apart into shards of smoke and fire. At last, her voice broke into nothingness.

When the storm clears, there is no trace of her. No body, no shadow, not even a whisper. Eris, the goddess of discord, is gone.
Swallowed by the chaos she thought she could control.

I stand alone in the silence that follows for a moment. Chest heaving. Eyes burning. For the first time in a long time, my life is my own.

The battlefield is still burning when I lower the encircling storm. The smoke curls in the air like mourning veils as I stand in the middle of the field. My breath ragged and my power from the storm calming to a trembling whisper.

Then I hear their voices. My loved ones are coming to find me. Through the haze, I see their figures appear. They are all calling my name. For a heartbeat, I cannot move. After so long being alone or under Eris's spell, after so much pain and fury, the sound of them caring feels almost unbearable.

My Olive runs to me first. She stops in front of me, tears streaking down her face. Her bright blue eyes meet mine. These are the eyes of my love. My mate. She smiles. Gods that smile. "You did it…you're free," she whispers as she cups my face with trembling hands.

My knees buckle before I realize what is happening. Olive is there with me and holds me close as the storm inside of me finally dies down.

"She's gone," I murmur, as I press my forehead to hers, my voice raw. "It's over."

Mark steps beside me and places his hand on my shoulder. It's steady and grounding. It is strangely comforting. I will deal with that later.

"Welcome back, Mal," Mark says quietly. I give him a nod, still holding on to Olive.

Gluskap and Set walk up next. Olive and I stand, and she steps back with Mark. Set grabs me into a hard hug with a slap on the back. He steps back with a big, infectious smile.

"Maybe we need to stay out of Hathor's wine for a while," he jokes, elbowing me, earning an eyeroll from Olive.

Gluskap stands in front of me, hesitating for only a moment before pulling me into a fierce, wordless embrace. I freeze and slowly return the hug. A choked half laugh, half sob escapes me. For the first time in ages, I am not trapped and helpless. I am not just a god of chaos. I am a mate, a brother, a friend, a soul who has finally broken free.

"It's over. We can go home," Olive whispers as she reclaims her spot against my chest.

I look at them all, all of them believed in me even when I could not. A faint, tired smile broke across my face.

"Home," I echo, "Yeah…I think I remember what that feels like."

Chapter 30: Olive

Malsumis is never leaving my sight again. I know I had good reason to be confused, but my gods, I have missed him and his touch.

Set and Gluskap have left and will meet us later for a little party. As we prepare to return to the human realm, the air thickens. The world has stilled. It's as if everything is holding its breath here. Something is coming.

We all turn as lightning splits the sky. Malsumis holds tighter as he looks up in recognition.

"Zeus," he whispers to me.

Zeus suddenly stands before us, tall and broad shouldered. His skin glows with a faint golden tone, and his eyes are a deep electric blue. His long, wavy, silvery hair and full, well kept beard give him an air of both wisdom and wrath. I'm guessing he is here for the latter.

He hasn't even spoken, but his presence is heavy with energy like an unbroken storm. The judgment burning in his eyes has the newfound calm I feel quaking beneath its weight.

"Eris is gone," Zeus thundered. "Balance must be kept. Her end demands a price."

"You would punish us for something she did?" Malsumis asks as he pushes me behind him.

"I was not fond of Eris, but the fact remains that balance must and will be kept. It is not punishment," Zeus counters.

"I will pay for upsetting the balance then. I was the one who killed Eris," Malsumis offers, as I begin to panic. I just got him back. I can't lose him again.

"Ha, no. I will not be upsetting the peace between your father and me."

"I am sure my father does not care for me," Malsumis says.

"Boy, you know nothing. He does more than you know. Anyway, you, your mate, and Set are favored by Ra, and I do not feel like crossing him today either. So that leaves the mortal."

"NO!" I scream and come out from behind Malsumis.

Malsumis goes to protect Mark, but it's too late. Zeus sends a lightning bolt through Mark's chest.

Mark falls to his knees as Maslsumis catches him, and I run to his side. He looks at me, stunned as I sob.

"Please stay with me. Don't leave, okay. Mark, I forbid you from leaving me."

"I love you, baby. I always have. Don't worry, it doesn't even hurt," he manages to get out in broken breaths.

"Mark, you must stay. You came here to save me. I will find a way to save you, too." Malsumis promises.

"It's okay, Mal. Take care of our girl." Mark says, before turning back to me and smiling one last charming smile. He closes his eyes and doesn't open them again.

"No. No. No. Mark. Please. Come back. Please. Come back." I cry.

"Zeus, bring him back now!" Malsumis snarls as he charges Zeus.

"Balance must be kept. The price has been paid," is all Zeus says before he and Mark disappear.

Chapter 31: Olive

I feel like a piece of my soul has been ripped from my being. I sit here where just a few moments ago I was holding Mark in my arms. My arms are now empty, and I am too stunned to move or make a sound. I look up at Malsumis, and he is just as horrified. He looks down at me with unshed tears in his eyes, and my dam breaks. I scream loud enough to wake the heavens and make the ground beneath us tremble. I crumple to the ground, and Malsumis grabs me and pulls me tightly against him. I scream and sob into his chest as he cries with me.

"Okay, we have…been…waiting…What's going on? Where's Mark?" Set's joking quickly turns serious.

"Zeus. He killed him." Malsumis says as he holds me, stroking my hair.

"No, no, no. That cannot be! Zeus did not even care for Eris!"

"I will explain later. Can we use the rooms in your palace?"

"Of course. Let's get Olive settled in your room." Set says sounding like he is on the brink of breaking.

I can hear them, but nothing is registering. All I can focus on is this empty hole in my heart. I am in so much pain. Not just emotion, actual physical pain. He can't be gone.

Malsumis picks me up, and the next thing I know, we are in Set's private rooms. Malsumis takes me to our room and sits me in a chair. He kneels in front of me.

"I am going to draw you a bath, and we are going to rest as much as we can, ok, my Love." I manage a weak nod.

He returns for the bathroom and gathers me in his arms. He helps me undress and step into the warm water. He follows in after me. He soaps the cloth and washes my body as I sit, staring into space. He lathers shampoo into my hair and massages it onto my scalp. It feels so good, I only wish I could enjoy it.

"I need you to lean back so I can rinse your hair, my Love."

I obey. When he is finished, he leans down and kisses my head. He pulls me against him, and we sit like that until the water cools. He gets out, wraps himself in a towel, and then helps me out of the water and towels me off. He helps me into a light gown that I wore when I was here before and leads me back to our room. I sit on the bed, and he climbs in behind me, beginning to brush my hair. He then braids it for me. "Can I hold you, my Olive?"

"Please," I beg.

He lies back and pulls me into him. I breathe in his earthy scent and soak in the warmth of his body as it wraps around mine. We lie here with my quiet cries into the pillow, the only sounds. I slowly drift off to sleep, my only release from the pain, or so I believe.

I open my eyes, and I am back in Malsumis field. Mark is standing feet from me. He looks at me with that beautiful smile. I reach for him, but I can't move. The air is thick. Heavy. The sky cracks with lightning, which blinds me momentarily. Mark comes back into view, and he looks confused. He calls my name. His eyes search for me in terror. I am trying to get to him, but I don't get there before a bolt of lightning strikes him through his chest.
All I can do is watch, powerless to save him.

"He is the price."

I jolt awake and scream. Malsumis is not beside me. I panic. I can't breathe. I am alone. Everyone is gone.

Malsumis and Set rush into the room, having heard my screams.

Malsumis runs to me, gathering me in his arms.

"I am here, my Love. I am so sorry."

"Please don't leave me. Please stay."

"I am never going anywhere. I only went to inform Set of our situation. I love you so much, Olive. I am here, love, I am here."

"I couldn't reach him in time…he looked at me right before…he was so scared…I couldn't save him." I say through my sobs.

"I know, my Love. We were not expecting the attack. I am so sorry I could not save him. I tried, I promise I tried."

"I know you did. This is Zeus's fault." I say with clarity.

"Olive," Set warns.

"How do you kill a Titan?"

Chapter 32: Malsumis

"It can't be done," Set says.

"I am sorry, my Olive, he is right. Titans cannot be killed."

"What about banished? Imprisoned?" Olive continues.

"The only one that has ever come close to defeating Zeus in any way was Typhon, and he is trapped under Mount Etna to this day. Before you get any ideas, Mal and I fought that monster, and he is worse than Zeus." Set explains to Olive.

"So I was powerless against saving Mark, and now I am powerless against avenging his death." Olive buries her face into my shoulder. "I am in pain, not just my emotions. I am in physical pain."

I look at Set, and he looks wide eyed back at me. It cannot be. Could Olive have two mates? Is that why they were drawn together like Olive and I were? Is this why I am feeling immense sadness as well? He was not my mate, but if he were Olive's, we would be connected as well through a bond. I nod to Set, and he knows exactly what I need him to do. Find someone with answers.

"What does your pain feel like, love?"

"It hurts everywhere. Like a piece of my soul has been ripped from me," she cries.

"I do not want to hurt you further, but I also do not want to keep anything from you." She looks up at me with those beautiful blue eyes, and for a second, I have to look away. "For you to feel a pain like this, Mark may have been your mate."

"But you're my mate, I feel it."

"He was mortal, you wouldn't have known until…" I trail off; we both know the rest of the explanation.

"What am I supposed to do, Malsumis? I can't live like this."

"The missing piece will always be there, from what I understand, but you will get used to it being there."

"If he even was one of my mates."

"Correct, Love."

"This is a lot to process."

"I am here to help you."

"Even after I refused you and caused you to be trapped again?"

"None of that was your fault. You had every right to push me away. Eris took advantage of that." I look away for a second, but Olive notices.

"What is it? You keep looking away from me? Did I do something?"

"No! You are perfect. I am okay."

"Are you really?"

"I am upset about Mark. I tried to intervene."

"Even if you had, Zeus would have just struck again. He came for payment, and he took it," she said coldly. I rest my head on hers and just hold her.

There is a knock at the door. Set walks in and sits down heavily in a chair. He and Mark had gotten close in the short time that they had known each other, and he is mourning his friend as well.

"Your brother is here. Is it okay if he comes in?"

"It is okay with me, as long as Olive is comfortable with it," she gives a nod, and Set calls Gluskap in.

"Set spoke with Thoth, and I spoke with Father, and both agree that Mark was most likely Olive's second mate. It is rare but not unheard of." Gluskap explains.

"I am surprised Father is not angry with you for helping me."

"It is quite the opposite. He said it was exactly the way things were supposed to happen. Unfortunately, so was Mark's mortal death. He was a good male. I am very sorry for the loss."

"What do you mean by mortal death?" Olive asks.

"That is just what Father said. Do you think that there could be more to it?" Gluskap asks.

"It is just an odd way to put it. Having met your father, he doesn't just say things that don't have deeper meaning." Olive answers.

"You are absolutely right. Let me see what I can find out. I will check back in with you after I try to get some answers from Father."

"Good luck with that, brother," I say as Gluskap gives me a quick hug.

"Thanks. I'm going to need it with him," he says with a laugh.

"I am going back to speak with Thoth about the meaning of this mortal death comment. I will be back." Set says, heading out the door, leaving Olive alone.

"Malsumis, the pain is gone," she says with questioning in her eyes.

"I have never heard of it going away like that. Let's take advantage of that and rest for a bit until Set gets back and we can get his thoughts on it." She hums in agreement and leans in to kiss me. I take a breath and pull back and kiss her forehead.

"What is wrong? Talk to me. You have never pulled away like that," she says with hurt in her eyes. How can I tell her what Eris made me do?

"I am just tired. We both need rest and to heal from all we have been through."

"Just don't push me away, my Love. I want to be there for you like you are there for me," she pleads.

"I love you, my Olive," I say as she snuggles onto my chest.

I know I should tell her what Eris did to me. She would understand and help me through it, but would she look at me differently? Would she think me a fool for being tricked so easily? I was so desperate to have Olive back that I just wanted her to love me again, and Eris knew that.

I cover my eyes with my arm, feigning to block out the light so Olive does not notice my tears of embarrassment.

Chapter 33: Olive

Something is going on with Malsumis. I intend on finding out what it is, too. We just found our way back to each other, and nothing is going to pull us apart again. He says he just needs rest, and while that is true, I didn't miss him silently crying himself to sleep.

His quiet, deep breaths let me know he is asleep. I place my hand on his temple and send soothing dreams to him. I slip out of bed and out of Set's rooms before anyone knows I am gone.

I transport myself to the doors of Ra's palace. If anyone can help me, it has to be him. His guard promptly blocks my way.

"Sorry, Goddess, Ra is not receiving visitors."

"I have to see him. Please, let me in."

"That cannot happen." The guard says, almost apologetically.

Suddenly, the doors burst open, and a burst of light blinds me.

As I am able to focus again, I see Ra silhouetted in the light.

"I thought I felt my favorite goddess's presence!" he turns toward the guard, "Always inform me of Olive's arrival."

"Yes, Your Éminence," the guard says as he bows low.

"Come, Olive, let us go to my gardens and speak privately."

I follow Ra into his gardens and am not prepared for what I see. Golden light pours over floating terraces overflowing with palm fronds and lotus blossoms over a river that looks like molten gold from the sunlight. Along the river, date trees and papyrus reeds rise with flowers I have never seen before. Where Ra walks, the ground brightens, and blossoms awaken as he passes. The air is humming with quiet power. This is the place where the dawn is born each day.

"I know this is no social visit. What brings you here, my beautiful creation?" Ra asks as he leads me to sit on a nearby bench.

"Well, apparently I have…had two mates," I say, trying not to choke up, "after Mark was killed, I felt like I was literally being ripped apart, but all of a sudden the pain stopped. Plus, Malsumis's father said something cryptic about a mortal death. What does this all mean?"

He lets out a breath and looks at me softly, "It can mean many things, Olive. He was never a true mate; he died a mortal death and came back, or even Zeus had mercy on you and blocked his passing on to the afterlife from you. When I heard of your mortal lover's passing, I tried to visit Zeus to obtain the body and bring him back as I did you, but Zeus has completely blocked communications with outside pantheons."

"Oh," I say softly and lower my head. Ra puts a finger under my chin and gently tilts my head up toward him.

"I will keep trying. In the meantime, keep trying to reach Malsumis. He has been through so much, and there is no telling what Eris did to him. She was the strongest spell caster I have ever seen and a vicious, vindictive one at that."

"He has been acting strange since he came back. I will do whatever I can to help him. I love him more than he will ever know."

"Oh, how I wish I could keep you for myself, but Malsumis deserves a win, so he shall keep his mate."

"What makes you think that I would ever leave him?" I sass, raising my brow to him.

"I can be quite…persuasive," he purrs. "For now, let us go deal with that mate who has currently kicked in the doors to my palace to get to you."

"What!" I exclaim as I jump from the bench I had been sitting on.

"Come along, I will take you to him," he says, very unbothered.

He holds his hand out for me to take. I hold his hand, and we go to the front of the palace. Malsumis and Set are there already, and when Malsumis sees my hand in Ra's, he looks ready to attack. "Stand down, Malsumis," Ra warns.

"Get away from her," Malsumis growls. I let go of Ra's hand and walk to Malsumis.

"He was just bringing me to you, my Love," I say calmly, taking Mal's hand in mine. He looks down at me and closes his eyes.

"I woke and could not find you. I panicked. The guard said you were with Ra and were not to be disturbed. I am sorry, my Olive." "You have nothing to apologize for. I am the one who is sorry for sneaking away while you were sleeping. I wanted you to rest, and I needed to speak with Ra."

"Since we are apologizing…I am sorry I dispatched your guard," Set says sheepishly.

"You killed the guard!" I say, shocked.

"He would not let us in," Set says, shrugging.

"Gods damn it, Set!" Ra scolds as he stomps off towards the doors.

"What? He will regenerate in a few hours," Set says, following his father out.

"Are you okay?" Malsumis asks quietly once we are alone.

"I am fine. I came to get answers about mortal death and why my pain suddenly stopped. I am so sorry I worried you." I wrap my arms around him, and he leans down and kisses my head.

"I was terrified something happened to you. When I realized you were here, I panicked that Zeus had come back for you, and Ra had to intervene. Then I saw your hand in Ra's. I do not want another male touching you. You are mine."

"I am yours, always. I promise he was only bringing me to you," I pull back, taking his hand in mine and kissing it. From where we are standing, we can hear Set and Ra arguing. "Let's go back to our room."

"If that is what you would like."

"You don't want to be alone with me, do you?" I ask, trying to hide the hurt in my voice. I failed.

"That is not what I mean. I am sorry. Of course, I want to be alone with you. I am not thinking straight," he says, trying to make me feel better.

"Let's go. We need to talk."

Chapter 34: Olive

We get back to our room and sit down in two chairs facing each other near the bookshelves.

"Have I done something to make you not want me?" I break the awkward silence between us.

"No, my Olive, you are the only thing that is good in my life. The only thing that kept me going in Eris's web of spells. Do not doubt this."

"Then please tell me what is going on. I know it is more than being tired. Even more than Mark being killed. Let me help you like you help me, my Love."

He puts his head in his hands. I rise from my seat and kneel in front of him, holding his hands in mine.

"Please let me in. I want to help you through this." I beg.

"I do not know how to tell you what I have been through. I want to, but I do not know how."

"It's okay. I am here. I am not going anywhere. I just want to love you. I want us to help each other heal from what Eris has put us through."

He looks at me with unshed tears in his eyes. I think he is going to tell me what has happened.

"I just need more rest. I am going to bed," he kisses my forehead and stands. "Malsumis…"

"I am tired. I need sleep," he says, and I know he is done.

"Okay. I will come lie with you."

"No…I mean, would you read to me like you used to?" He requests.

"Of course I will. I will do anything you need me to."

He climbs into bed and closes his eyes. I climb in beside him and begin to read to him. Before I know it, I hear his soft snores beside me. I close the book and place my hand close to his head so as not to wake him. I send soothing energies to him so he will be at peace in his dreams. I push his hair from his face and climb out of bed. As I pass the door, there is a light knock. I open the door, knowing it can only be Set.

"He is asleep," I whisper.

"Again?" Set says quietly.

I nod and gesture for Set to follow me back into his room. I take a deep breath and sit on his sofa facing his fireplace.

"Something happened with Eris, Set. Something horrible."

"He is acting differently. He has not told you?"

"No. He says he wants to, but doesn't know how. He can tell me anything. I don't understand." I begin to cry. Set sits beside me.

"I am sure he will tell you soon. Maybe he does need the rest and time to process."

"Maybe you're right. He won't even kiss me, hold me, or look at me hardly."

"I know this is a difficult time for both of you. I am sorry, Olive."

"I still have to go back and deal with everything with Mark's death. It has already been 2 months in the human realm. How am I going to explain that? I know he has no contact with his family, but what about our friends and work? How am I supposed to do all of this?"

"Do not worry, I have handled everything," Set says. I blink at him through my tears.

"What?"

"I quit his and your job for both of you. Texted your friends to let them know you had been accepted for a job starting immediately in Egypt. I paid off his house and car until you decide what you want to do with them. Mark was my friend, and I wanted to do something to help."

"Thank you, Set. I don't know how to thank you enough." I cry.

"Help Mal through this. Be patient with him. All he has ever wanted is a family that loved him unconditionally. He has that with us; he just needs to be shown that."

"Of course I will. I love him. I want to show him that."

"I know you do. I know you are still grieving, too. I am your friend too, Olive. I am here for you," Set says, putting his arm around me, pulling me into a hug. I hug him back and cry into his shoulder. I cry for Mark. I cry for Malsumis. I cry because I am lost in this moment.

Chapter 35: Malsumis

I know I should tell her. I need to tell her. I have to tell her.

How can I tell her when I cannot even say what Eris did to me to myself? My mate kneels in front of me, wanting to help me, begging to tell her so she can help.

I look at her through tears in my eyes.

I cannot tell her.

I make up an excuse about needing rest and panic when she suggests joining me. It's not that I do not want her to. I do. All I can think of is how stupid I was to let Eris trick me into being with her by pretending to be Olive.

I so enjoy her reading to me, though, and I let her angelic voice put me to sleep.

I have a peaceful sleep. Quiet. Calm. I have a feeling Olive had something to do with that. I wake to find Olive gone. I do not like this new habit of hers. I slide out of the bed and go to the door. I hear hushed voices from the other side. I crack the door and realize that it is Olive and Set. They are sitting too close on the sofa for my comfort. I realize Olive is crying. I listen in for a moment. She is crying for me. She is grieving for Mark. She has so much on her, and I am stressing her out even more. I am so selfish.

Right as I go to comfort her, Set pulls her into a hug. I begin to fill with rage. I start to barge in, but Olive's cries break through my anger. I have done this to her. I have to get past these feelings of anxiety, embarrassment, and stupidity. We need to reconnect, and I do not think we can do that here. I need to be somewhere just for Olive and me. We need to go back to our home in the human realm for a while.

I turn and go back to bed just before Olive comes back in quietly, sniffling. She climbs in beside me, careful not to touch me, and turns away from me. I turn toward her and go to put an arm around her to pull her in close. I need to be close to her. I freeze. Her quiet crying has turned into soft breaths of sleep. Instead, I climb out of the other side of the bed and visit Set.

I go into Set's room and find him with his head in his hands on his sofa. All of this is weighing heavily on him, too.

"Set?"

"Oh, sorry, Mal. I did not hear you come in. Where is Olive?"

"She is asleep. Thank you for comforting her. I should be the one to be doing so. I am keeping something from her, and my reaction to her keeps getting worse."

"She told me. She is worried about you…Eris did something. Something unspeakable," He says as a fact, like he already knows, so I only nod, letting him know he is right.

"How am I supposed to tell Olive? She will think I am a fool. A weak mate."

"You know that is not true, Mal. She will understand and do whatever it takes to help you through this. I believe she already suspects something like this has happened."

"You do? Yet she is still at my side…"

"She loves you, Mal."

"I think we need to go back to the human realm for a while."

"That may be a good idea. She needs to grieve for Mark and cannot fully do that here."

"Of course she does. I am a horrible, selfish mate. I only think of my own problems."

"No, you have been through trauma just like her. You both need to heal, and you need to do it together."

"When did you get so wise?"

"I have always been wise."

"A wise ass, maybe."

"There is my Mal."

We talk about warding the house to keep Olive protected and about getting Gluskap to help make sure the wards are as strong as they can be. We sit and talk for a while, and then I go back to Olive. I cannot believe she has slept this long.

I go back to our room and find that she, in fact, is awake and reading in front of the fire. I take a moment to admire her. So much has changed since the first time I saw her walk into that house. One thing that has not changed is that I am utterly obsessed with her. I walk up behind her and see that she has one of her 'spicy' books, as she calls them. Oh, naughty Olive. I kiss the top of her head, and she looks up at me with those beautiful, bright blue eyes. My Olive's eyes, not Eris's imitation.

"I love you, my Olive. You know that, right?"

"I do, but you are worrying me."

"I know, and I will do better." I sit beside her.

"You don't have to do better, love. I want to help you through this. You just have to let me in."

"I know. I will," I mean that too.

"Do you want me to read to you while you rest?"

"No, I actually want to ask you something."

"Okay…" she says, looking questioningly.

"I think we should go back to our house. I want to help each other through our troubles and reconnect, and I believe that is the best place to do so. If you do not want to, we can go somewhere else." "I agree. I think we need to be in our space."

"I am going to get my brother to help Set and me set up wards to make sure that the house is protected."

"That sounds good…"

"What is it?"

"I need to tell you something. I may have tried to go into Zeus's dreams, and it may have pissed him off," she looks at me sheepishly.

As if on cue, there are three hard knocks at Set's main doors.

"Shit," Olive and I say, looking at each other.

"OLIVE!" Ra's booming voice floods the room.

"Yes," she says innocently as Set and I move in front of her.

"Why did Zeus show up at my palace ranting about my dream goddess infiltrating his mind?"

"Well, because I did. I was trying to find out what he did with Mark," she said boldly.

"Olive," Ra says, pinching his brow, trying to look mad. "Look at that face, I cannot stay mad at you. Listen, my beautiful girl, you cannot be going into the mind of that Titan. You could get hurt. Now, my mind, you are welcome into anytime," he says with a wink.

I step closer to her and shoot Ra a look. He just laughs.

"Stand down, Malsumis. I know she is yours. You should have seen Zeus's face, though. I do not believe I have seen him so red or so disheveled. You really got to him, my little dreamer.”

“I am sorry for the inconvenience I caused you, but I had to try,” Olive says.

“I understand, dear. Please, for your sake, do not do that again,” with that, Ra is gone.

“Damn, Olive, Father really is smitten with you. He would have had my ass if I did something like that. We stole Zeus’s lightning bolt one time, and I thought he was going to kill Mal and me.” Set says.

“Well, too bad for him, I am happily taken,” she says, looking up at me. I cannot help but smile back at her.

Chapter 36: Olive

It has been four months in the human realm since I lost Mark. I still have not faced it properly. I don't know if it is possible to. I feel him still, even though I know he is gone. It is like somehow he is just going to be there when I turn around. We are moving back into our house today, and I am ready to heal and move forward with Malsumis.

The guys are finishing up setting up wards while I grab some pizza. They eat a ton in their human forms, which is mainly just shorter versions of themselves with dimmer magic. Seven foot god would stand out just a little. Malsumis did not want me to go alone, but I insisted…adamantly and loudly.

I am about to get in my car when I hear my name being called. It's Jennifer.

"Bitch! Why didn't you tell us you were back in town?" she says as she pulls me in for a hug.

"I just got back. I am just getting settled."

"That's a lot of pizza for you and Mark. You're having a party and didn't invite me?" She laughs.

"Mark and I broke up," I say, tearing up.

"Oh no! Olive, I am so sorry! Do I need to kick his ass?"

"No, no. We just wanted different things and agreed it wasn't going to work out."

"So, who is all the pizza for? Should we have a girls' night?"

"Well, I have some friends I met helping me move in, but you are welcome to come over. We have plenty."

"I don't want to impose."

"You guys are my best friends. You're not imposing."

"I will grab Candy and will be over in a bit then!"

"Sounds great!"

We hug, then I head home. I hope the boys don't mind company.

I get home, and the guys inhale five of the six pizzas I brought home. I manage to save one for us girls. Jennifer and Candy get there and are smitten with the boys right away. Insert eyeroll. Set and Gluskap certainly do not mind the attention. Of course, we don't use their real names. So, Set is Seth, Gluskap is Kap, and Malsumis is Mal. As far as the girls know, I met them at the dig site in Egypt, we all came back together, and they are renting Mark's house.

"So Mal, what brings you back to the States?" Jennifer asks flirtatiously.

"Olive," he says plainly and slides his arm around my waist. Gods his touch feels good.

"OH! Well done, Olive!" Jennifer exclaims, which earns her a chuckle from Malsumis.

"Thanks, I think I lucked out with him," I say, looking up at his handsome face. He smiles back at me.

"It is I who is the lucky one, Love." There is heat in the look he gives me. For the first time in a while, I see my Mal.

"Ugh, gag. Anyway, Halloween is coming up. What are we doing?"

"Oh, I haven't thought about it. My last one wasn't so great."

"More of a reason we have to make this birthday great!" Candy walks up and exclaims.

"I have thought about this. We will be Beauty and the Beast." Malsumis speaks up.

"You thought about this? Beauty and the Beast?"

"It is your favorite animation, right?"

"It is. I am just surprised you remembered." "I remember everything about you."

"Awwwwww," Candy says.

"Gross," Set and Jennifer say at the same time, while Gluskap just chuckles.

Later in the evening, while everyone is chatting in the kitchen, I pull Kap aside. The nickname is growing on him.

"What did you ever find out from your father about mortal death?" I ask.

"Not much. It is just as it sounds. He could have died and been brought back, but it does not look like that happened. Zeus sent him to Tartarus. Mark is Hades's property now. Hades does not let anyone out easily."

"But it isn't impossible."

"Olive, do not do whatever it is you are thinking. Hades is not one to be trifled with."

"I will not do anything to put myself or Mal into harm's way."

"Good. Let's go join the others before Malsumis thinks I have stolen you away."

We both are laughing when we enter the kitchen. Malsumis looks murderous. Oops. I go to him, and he puts an arm around my shoulders and kisses my head. That contact grounds him, and he calms. Coming home was the right move. Every moment, he feels more like my Malsumis.

The night wraps up, and everyone heads their separate ways. As soon as the door closes, Malsumis is close to me. I feel the heat coming from his body. Gods, I want him so bad. Does it make me a bad person that I am grieving one mate and still want the other?
Before I can question it further, he speaks.

"What did Gluskap want with you?"

"It was me who asked him to step out of the room. I was asking him about Mark."

"What did he say?" Malsumis asks as he pushes the hair from my shoulders.

"That Mark is in Tartarus with Hades and that Hades would not let him go."

"That is correct. No one escapes Tartarus."

I look at him with tears in my eyes.

"Oh, my Olive, I am so sorry. If I thought I could retrieve him, I would. I feel some of the grief you feel. I cannot imagine how it is for you," he says. Malsumis looks down at me and captures my lips with his in a slow, timid kiss. I answer back with one of my own, and he becomes more needy and heated. He pushes me back into the wall, and his hands begin to roam over my body like he is remembering all my curves. Suddenly, he pulls back with something that is almost fear in his eyes.

"Hey, my Love, it's okay. What is it? Are you okay?" I ask.

"I am sorry. I am so sorry, my Olive," he says quickly and heads up to our room.

"Malsumis, wait! Please tell me what is going on," I beg as I follow him upstairs. When I go into the room, I find him pacing.

"I am so sorry, Olive. I thought she was you. She tricked me."

"What do you mean, my Love?" I am trying to stay calm, but I am beginning to think I know what Eris did to my mate.

"I ignored the signs. I missed you so much that I ignored the wrongness and let her trick me. I didn't want to have sex with her. I remember my body reacting as something in my mind was screaming it was wrong. I am so sorry, my Olive." His voice fractures. My mate, who has fought gods and nearly torn apart kingdoms, is breaking. "I swear to you I did not choose it. Please believe me." His strength fails him, and he falls to his knees. I rush over to him, and he wraps his arms around me. "Please, forgive me. Please."

"There is nothing to forgive because you did nothing wrong. She did that to you. You did nothing wrong, my Love. Please know that," I say on repeat as I hold him crying.

"My mind his broken. I question every craving. Every touch. Is it my Olive? Or is this still her?"

"I am your Olive, Malsumis. Look," I raise my sleeve to reveal the feather tattoo that he drew on my skin. "She didn't know about this. I am your Olive. This is real, not a spell. You are free. I am your mate, and you are mine. I love you so much."

He takes my arm in his hands and inspects my tattoo by running his fingers over it. He looks at me with tears starting to slow.

"My Olive."

"Always yours."

He presses his forehead to mine, and we stay like this for several minutes, just connecting in silence.

"I am sorry I kept this from you. I just feel so stupid. I am embarrassed. I thought you would think that I wanted it."

"You have nothing to apologize for. I have been where you are, and we all have to process in our own ways."

"I do not mean to push you away. It is difficult to be too close right now. I am trying."

"You set the pace, and I will follow your lead. I will never push you to do anything you are not ready for. I just want to be here for you and to love you."

"I love you, my Olive. We will heal together. We will come out stronger than before."

"You are absolutely right. I love you, Malsumis."

Chapter 37: Malsumis

"A date?" I repeat.

"Yes, a date. Like dinner and a walk or dinner and a movie. A date!" Olive says excitedly.

"Olive, would you like to go on a date with me?" I say with a smirk.

"YES! I need to go pick out an outfit!"

"You know you can just use your power to create one, right?"

"Yes, Captain Obvious. I just don't want you to see before it's time to go!" she says, running up the stairs. I lean into the foyer and watch her plump bottom go upstairs. Gods, I love that woman and her curves.

It has been two weeks since I told Olive what happened with Eris, and slowly, I am becoming more myself around her. I was so scared she would think I was weak and unworthy of her love. That has been my experience in the past, especially with the humans, but she has proven me wrong. She truly loves me unconditionally, and that means everything to me. I am still cautious with my touch, and she has not pushed me. We sleep in the same bed, but we do not hold each other as we once did.

I do not like it, and I want to remedy this. I am hoping tonight I can get close to her again in more ways than just that.

While Olive gets ready, I get ready myself. I dress in a black button-up shirt, black pants, and black shoes, and I pull my hair back. There, easy…now I wait. Olive always insists that she needs to look perfect, but I think she already looks perfect as she is, so I do not understand why she insists on it. She is worth the wait, though. So, I wait. I pick up Olive's phone and look up places to take her. There is a spot right outside of the town called "The Loft". It has many food options, games, and dancing. This is what we need to get our minds off our troubles.

"Okay, are you ready for the big reveal?" Olive calls from the staircase.

"Absolutely," I say with a smile, walking to the bottom of the stairs. I look up at her as she comes down. She is wearing a black dress that hugs all her lovely curves perfectly and black boots up to her knees, leaving just enough skin to tease me. Her hair lies in soft waves cascading down over her shoulders and down her back.

Words catch in my throat as I take in her beauty.

"Is it bad? I can change," she says when I take too long to comment.

"No, quite the opposite, my Olive. You have no idea what you look like, do you?" I ask, voice rough with awe. "You were made with things the universe only whispers about. Even I, who has seen worlds reborn, have never seen such beauty until I met you. You are the kind of beauty that undoes gods." I take a step closer and put my hand out for her to take. I see her tattoo. Not Eris. I look into those bright blue eyes, and she smiles. A smile that feels like a dawn breaking after centuries of storm.

"Me, beautiful? You, my Love, my beautiful chaos, your eyes hold something wild, endless, alive. You bend the storm of chaos to your will, yet there is stillness in you. The kind that only exists between thunder and lightning. Your beauty undoes me, Malsumis."

No one has ever described my chaos as beautiful before. Most run from it. Despise it. Try to control it. She just loves me. I tilt her face up gently and capture her lips with mine. The kiss is tender, lingering. There is no rushing. She lets me lead with slow exploration. This kiss says everything. It is not about passion. It is about trust and affection. We part, and I put my forehead to hers.

"I love you, my Olive."

"I love you, my warrior."

"I do love that name," I say with a grin. "Now, it is time for our date. I found the perfect place. I will drive."

"Whoa, whoa, whoa…you have never driven! You were trapped when cars were invented!"

"I am a god, Olive. How hard can it be?"

It turned out to be more difficult than I had estimated. Much to my humiliation, and after many, many laughing fits from Olive, she took over.

When we get to 'The Loft', Olive gets too quiet. Something is wrong.

"My Olive, what is wrong?"

"Nothing."

"It is definitely something, I can feel it."

"Well, Mark and I used to come here with our friends."

"Oh, Olive, I did not know. I am sorry. We can go somewhere else. Anywhere else."

"You couldn't have known. It's okay. I have to get used to being in this realm without him."

"Are you sure?"

"Yes, I'm sure. Besides, I need to see how bad you are at bowling after seeing you drive," she says with a smile. It doesn't go unnoticed that it doesn't reach her eyes, though. This night will be about her healing, and I am more than willing to help her through this.

Chapter 38: Olive

"Oh, I'm a god, I can drive a car, Olive…" I say while laughing my ass off.

"Oh yes, so hilarious. Go ahead and laugh, Love, you pay for that later." Malsumis jokes.

"Oooo so scary!" I sass back, "Promises, promises."

When I realize where we are going, I get quiet. I feel like I may burst into a sob. Oh gods, how am I going to do this? Malsumis asks if I want to go somewhere else, and I honestly do, but I need to do this. I haven't gone to Mark's house yet. I just can't. I have to do this; I can't hide from losing him forever.

As we walk in, Malsumis takes my hand into his, and the contact grounds me. I can do this. We head to the arcade area first. Maybe the games will help me get my mind off things.

"Why don't we test your bowling skills, my big bad warrior?" I tease.

"I know bowling. There was a male who watched it many years ago at our house. I can play this with ease," he answers confidently.

"Your confidence is…cute," I say, messing with him.

"I am not…*cute*. I am a warrior. Warriors are not *cute*," he says seriously.

"Ooooh, my bad, Mr. Big, Strong Warrior," I say with a giggle.

"I am *your* warrior, my Olive," he says into my ear, sending shivers all over my body. I look into his deep onyx eyes, and they are full of a heat I haven't seen in what feels like forever.

"If you keep looking at me like that, I am going to be too distracted to beat your ass at bowling," I say softly back. That earns me a laugh. Gods, I have missed that sound.

"You can try, Love. I fear you underestimate me," he says with an infectious smile.

We start our game, and he immediately gets a strike. He turns and looks at me with his hands in his pockets and a grin on his face.

"Did you just use your power?" I say in a whisper, yell. He just keeps that reckless grin, with his hands in his pockets, and shrugs. I don't know if I want to smack him or make out with him. Wait, I do know…totally make out with him. He looks gorgeous and so carefree right now.

"Your turn, my goddess," he says as he walks past me to sit. Oh, two can play this game!

I shake my head and step up for my turn. I take a breath and quieten all the chatter of the people around us. I let my ball go, and it glides perfectly. The pins sway as if caught in a slow breeze, and one by one they fall.

"Elegant cheating. I am impressed."

"It's called finesse, my big, strong warrior. Unlike your…gravitational brute force," I say innocently. "Ouch, you wound me."

"Not yet, but if you cheat again, I might," I tease.

He laughs, a low, warm sound that makes the air around us hum with his power. After I am done admiring him, I go to turn and find my shoelace untied. I pause and narrow my eyes at him.

"Did you just…"

"Gravity must have slipped again," he says, feigning innocence.

He steps up for his turn, and I lean down to tie my laces and whisper to the ball. It stops inches in front of the pins, refusing to move. He looks back at me, and I have to hide my smile.

"So much for not cheating. You make the subtle look dangerous."

"You make danger look tempting, my warrior."

For a breath, it feels like everything in the alley seems to hold its breath around us. Then all the pins crash to the floor around us at once. All the people are cheering, none the wiser.

"We make a good team." Malsumis says smiling.

"Or a terrible one with all the cheating," I comment.

"I say skip the score keeping and get burgers and milkshakes instead," he says.

"Only if you promise to quit whispering to physics."

"No promises, my Olive."

Chapter 39: Malsumis

I know that being here at 'The Loft' is not easy for Olive, even though she is doing her best to hide the pain. I suggest that we leave and go to a diner I saw on the way here. I have seen places like this on television, but never in person. It is what the mortals call a retro diner. Neon lights and music from a jukebox greet us as we walk in. The hostess shows us to our seats, and we slide into the red vinyl booth.

Olive carefully studies the menu, and I lean back and study her.

I stretch an arm lazily over my side of the booth.

"You know," I say with a grin, "for someone who can decide the dreams of others, you seem to be having a difficult time deciding between a chocolate and vanilla milkshake."

"You always choose chaos and mischief," she teases with a soft laugh.

"I will always choose you, my Olive."

"Ok, you flirt," she teases again and sets down the menu. "I choose strawberry."

The waiter walks up, none the wiser that he is in the presence of a goddess and a god, and smiles as he takes my order. Then he turns to Olive, and his eyes linger too long for my liking. He takes her order and leaves the table.

"I did not like how he looked at you."

"Oh, he is probably trying to get a bigger tip."

"I will give him a tip."

"Mal…"

"What?" I say innocently. She smirks and shakes her head.

I see the waiter bringing our shakes, and suddenly, he trips. He falls back, and the milkshakes go all over his head and chest.
Oops.

"MALSUMIS!" Olive whisper yells at me, gods, she is so cute when she's mad. "Did you do that to him?"

"I may have had something to do with it," I say nonchalantly, shrugging.

"See choosing chaos and mischief."

"See, choosing you. His eyes lingered too long on what is mine."

"Oh gods, you're impossible. You know that, right?"

"Impossibly handsome."

"Ugh, that too," she laughs.

The kitchen sends our burgers and new shakes out with the hostess who sat us. The meal is perfect in its mortal simplicity. I bite into my burger. I have had one before, but it was nothing like this.

"Mortals," I say with my mouth full, "really understand simple pleasures."

"They do have their moments," she agrees. Olive then licks a trace of shake from her lips, and I nearly forget how to breathe, remembering what it feels like to have her mouth, her tongue, on me.

"That milkshake is now my mortal enemy," I joke.

"What? Why?" she laughs.

"It is where I want to be, on your tongue."

The next thing I know, there is a French fry flying at me. I look at her in surprise, and she just laughs.

"You're so bad," she says.

"I can be."

"Did you come here just to flirt?"

"You got me. The burgers were just a cover," that earns me one of her heavenly giggles.

"So we went bowling and had dinner. What is next for our date?"

"I was thinking we could go home and watch a movie like we used to."

"That sounds perfect!" She says excitedly, then gets serious. "Who is choosing the movie, though?"

"You can, Love," I say with a chuckle. "Let's go."

A smile breaks out across her beautiful face. A smile that I used to wish was just for me now is. I vow in this moment to always make her smile every day.

As we leave the restaurant, I slip my hand into hers. She looks up at me, a little surprised, and then gives me a slight squeeze but says nothing. I open the car door for her.

"Tomorrow, we begin driving lessons. I will learn to drive this thing."

"Absolutely, we will. I can't have my big, strong warrior being the passenger princess all the time," she laughs as I let out a fake, annoyed groan. I am still smiling as I slide into my side of the car.

On the ride home, we chat about what movie we will watch. Olive says that we will compromise and watch a superhero movie with romance and action. Honestly, it does not matter to me as long as I am with her. Tonight has been precisely what we needed to connect and relax. We make it home, and Olive says she will get changed so we can start the movie.

"Your power makes that much easier to change," I comment.

"I know, but doing little things like this keeps me connected to who I was before."

She says innocently and casually, but it stabs me like a dagger to the heart. It is my fault she is different. She did not mean it that way at all, but it is the truth. I stand at the bottom of the stairs as she enters our room to change. I go upstairs and stand in our doorway. Her back is to me. Gods, she is gorgeous. I watch as she lets her dress drop to the floor. The moonlight paints her glowing skin. I walk up behind her, and she stills. I gently push her hair from her shoulder and lean down to breathe her in…my Olive.

She leans her head to one side as I begin kissing her neck. My hands dance across the curves of her waist, and I slowly turn her around to face me. She looks up at me with heat in those brilliant blue eyes.

"Are you sure?" she asks softly.

"Yes. I need you."

"I will let you lead."

I capture her lips in a kiss full of everything I cannot express with words. She matches my eagerness as I back her to the bed. I remove her bra while I pepper her chest with kisses. I take her nipple in my mouth, and she rewards me with one of her beautiful breathy moans…my Olive. I take my time kissing across her chest before I take her other breast in my mouth. She goes to put her hands in my hair and pauses. I reach up and guide her to finish her action. Her fingers gently wrap into my hair as she tilts her head back in pleasure.

I continue feathering kisses down the soft skin of her stomach until I realize she has no panties on. Oh, my naughty Olive. I look up at her, and she puts her hand on the side of my face, letting me know I am in control. I see the tattoo on her arm…my Olive.

In one quick motion, I lay her on her back on the bed and push her thighs apart.

"Remember when I said you would pay for that sassy mouth of yours?"

"Yes," she says needily.

I form tendrils of shadows and wrap them on each wrist, pulling her arms above her head and then around her ankles, spreading her legs apart for me.

"Now you will pay, my Olive."

"Malsumis," she says heavily.

I run my fingers down her body, slowly taking my time, relearning every perfect curve. She squirms under my touch. I reach the apex of her thighs, and I look up at her.

"Oh, Olive, it has been too long since I have had you. Can I take my time?"

"Yes," is all she can manage between her heavy breaths.

That is all I need to hear. I kiss the inside of her thigh and then taste her. Oh gods, she tastes better than I remember. Fuck taking my time. I begin licking her like a male starved.

"Malsumis…fuck."

I grin against her. I push two fingers inside of her and hit the spot that drives her wild. I suck on her clit while continuing to fuck her with my fingers.

"Mal…I'm gonna…come…oh MALSUMIS," she screams as she comes on my face. Fresh wetness coats my fingers, which I greedily lick.

"Olive, you are still my favorite meal. Now what to do with you?"

"Malsumis…please…" she pants.

"Please, what, my Olive?"

"Fuck me, please. I need you."

Who am I to deny her when she asks so nicely? I release the shadows holding her ankles so she can move her legs. I line up my cock to her entrance and slowly push into her. Both of us moan out in how fucking good this feels. I pull back and start slowly fucking her.

"Harder, Mal, please, fuck me harder."

Gods, she undoes me. I pull back and thrust in as hard as I can. She sharply intakes and moans. It is like a dam breaks, and I become wild and erratic and fuck her until we are both screaming out in pleasure.

I release her arms from the shadow holds, and she brushes the hair from my face. I lean down and kiss her deeply.

"Can I take care of you now, Olive?"

"Let's take care of each other."

I have her wait on the bed as I draw us a bath. We bathe together and then crawl into bed and fall asleep in each other's arms. For once in what seems like forever, everything is right for us.

Chapter 40: Mark

I'm falling into the darkness. All I remember is Zeus striking me, then Olive and Mal over me, crying. Olive. My sweet girl. Will I ever see her again?

Suddenly, I am on solid ground. There is no light here. The air is heavy and oppressive with dread. My eyes adjust to the darkness, and I see light in the distance, so I walk toward it. I look up at the sky, if you can call it that, and it is nothing but swirling clouds the color of bruises. The ground I am walking on is cracked and glowing, as if veins of magma flow just below the surface. The closer I get to the light I saw, the more I realize it is walls made of fire. I hear voices, screams, and whispers of those trapped and bound in molten iron behind the walls. From behind the bars of molten iron and fire, I see twisted spirits and monsters. I swear I hear Eris's laughter and whispered voice.

"You will take my place…if you are strong enough. You will wear my crown."

I don't answer. My resolve is stronger than anything this place can throw at me. I have to get back to Olive.

I continue walking until I come upon three women…weaving. Oh shit, these are the fates. My area of concentration in college was Greek mythology, so I know exactly what they are doing. The three sisters sit in a circle around their weaving, the threads of life. The youngest of the three, Clotho, is at the spindle and looks the kindest of the three. The next sister, who I assume is Lachesis, looks calm and deliberate as she measures out the threads. The oldest of the three, Atropos, looks stern, with a pair of shears in her hand. A shiver runs through me, knowing that those shears mean the end of someone's life. One of the sisters looks directly at me. I'm fucked.

"I am Clotho. You were not meant to be here, Mark."

"Send me back."

"That cannot be done," she says. I look down in disappointment.

"But we can turn you into something more."

"What do you mean? What if I don't want to?"

"You want to get back to your love?"

"I will get back to her."

"Then this is the only way for you to pass the trials. We have seen this."

"Trials? You know that I will do it. Anything to get back to my girl."

The sisters uncovered what appears to be a stone well in the center of where they were sitting.

"Get in," Atropos says sternly.

"You want me to get into a dark pit?"

"Do you want to get back to her?" Lachesis asks.

"More than anything."

"Then get in," Atropos says, patience wearing thin.

This time I obey. I may have questions, but I'm not an idiot. This female could end me on the spot. I climb in, and the well comes just above my head, so I am fully covered in the hole. The sisters surround the well, and I see that Atropos has put her shears down. I know exactly what they mean by making me into something different now. Clotho has spun golden thread, and Lachesis is measuring it above me. They are reweaving my lifespan. They begin to chant ancient words I don't understand. A blinding pain sears throughout my body, and I scream out. The pain continues as light builds in the pit, extending upward, blocking out the sisters. As suddenly as the pain began, it ends. I feel different. Still me, but changed.

"Rise from the pit," commands Atropos. I do as she requests, and as I do, I notice tattoos of chains wrapping around my arms that are glowing faintly.

"You are now Markus the Reforged. Let your mortal heart and divine power guide your way back to your mate." Lachesis announces.

"Mate? Olive is my mate? She has a mate already."

"On rare occasions, gods are blessed with two mates; such is your case, Markus. Go now before Zeus realizes what we have done here today. You will face three trials. If you pass, you have a chance to make it back to your love." Clotho explains.

"What do you mean by a chance?"

"It will be out of our hands. This is Hades's realm," and without a goodbye, the sisters are gone.

Chapter 41: Mark

With the sisters gone, I am left alone with only the distant screams and whispers to keep me company. They said this is Hades's realm, which means I'm in Tartarus. Fuck. According to mythology, Hades doesn't let anyone leave here. Well, I guess it's not mythology. How did I end up here? I mean, obviously, Zeus threw me here when he killed me, which I am still salty about. But a year ago, I had no clue gods really existed. Places like this didn't really exist to me. I only believed in what I could prove through my work. Now here I am, a gods damn immortal. A fucking god myself.

Sometime during my whole inner monologuing, I stumbled through this wasteland of ash and came up on a river. I see a boat docked on the side of the banks with a cloaked figure inside. Charon. The Ferryman. So, this must be the River Acheron, the river of woe and pain. This keeps getting better and better. I approach him.

"A coin to cross," a raspy voice says.

"I don't have a coin."

"Then you do not cross."

"I have to get across. Apparently, I am supposed to go through trials, so I can try to get out of here."

"Ah, this begins your three trials."

"Ooookay, so how do I get across if you won't take me?"

"Swim," and with that, he begins to leave me on the shore alone.

"Fucking great," I murmur to myself, raking my hand through my hair.

I step back and take in the black river shimmering with faint, dying lights. I bend down and touch the water, and it ripples with voices. Voices of my past. Voices of my parents disowning me because I told them I was gay. I hear the voices of past relationships where I wasn't good enough to keep. I hear Olive crying over me while I was dying, begging me to stay. I see the faces of those I love, the ones I feel like I failed. The one I lost, my goddess.

"You cannot carry love into the depths," the current whispers.

It's now or never. I begin to wade into the shallows of the river. As soon as I get into the water, I feel the immense sadness spreading through my body. Once I am in the water, I can see souls floating past. No, not floating. The current is carrying them. As they try to fight it, I hear their cries. I have to keep moving forward. Soon, my cries join in the chorus around me. Every happiness I have ever felt is being stripped from me, memory by memory.

Just as I am reaching the shore, something pulls me under. I struggle to free myself. I break the surface, gasping, and am pulled under again. This time I see what has me leg. It is the soul of a woman. A human. While the others around us sink with their grief, she is fighting back. I feel the pulse of her defiance through all of the sorrow. The river has tested her resolve just as it has mine, and she still fights. I reach down to her.

"Only one may survive," the current murmurs.

"But she fights, she is aware. I can't leave her."

"If you wish to survive, you must," the river answers.

To save myself, I have to condemn this woman to an eternity of torturous sadness. I scream out in pain. In anger. In infinite sadness for what I am about to do. I will do whatever it takes to get back to Olive. I reach down and pry her hand from my leg. All the while, she is calling for me to stop, begging me to save her, clawing at me to get a better grip. I finally get away from her grip. She grabs me again, not as tightly this time. I kick her away from me. This time, the current pulls her away. She screams and fights the entire time. I scream I'm sorry until I can speak no longer.

By the time I reach the far bank, my tears are gone. My heart is hollow. My will to get back to Olive is the only thing that remains.

Chapter 42: Olive

It's been six months since I lost Mark; this time last year, we were getting ready for Christmas together. I miss him so much. I have good days and bad. Malsumis has been amazing and supportive through them all. Today I am in desperate need of a distraction. So we invited Set and Gluskap over to help decorate for our Christmas dinner tomorrow with all of us, Jennifer, and Candy.

"We need a dying tree," Set announces.

"It's just called a Christmas tree, and we had one until you set it on fire," I tease.

"Don't worry, I am on it!" Gluskap says before he disappears.

"I will hang our socks over the fireplace," Malsumis offers.

"Stockings, they're called stockings."

"Oh, that is right, you would think that I would be used to that by now, after how many of these traditions I have seen."

"I am back with our dead tree!" Gluskap says happily.

"Christmas tree, brother," Malsumis corrects.

"I found the eggnog, and I improved it!" Set exclaims and hands me a glass.

"Set! This is straight rum!" I manage to get out after the surprise burn.

"You say that like it is a bad thing," he says.

"No, just a shock," I say, taking another drink.

"Let us drink and be merry, Olive!" Set says, putting his arm around my shoulder.

"Set," Malsumis growls.

"Oh, Mal, settle down. Olive is my bestie. Well, unless she wants to take me up on my countless offers to include me in your bed…" Set looks at me expectantly.

"The answer is still no, Set," I laugh.

"You can't blame me for…what is it that the mortals say? Shooting my shot." I just roll my eyes at him while he laughs.

"I'm going to help Kap with the lights on the tree," I say.

"I will help too," Set says.

"Oh no, you won't," Malsumis speaks up. "You set the damn thing on fire last time."

"Some God of Chaos you are, Mal! A little excitement never hurt anyone."

"My chaos days are over. I just want to be settled with Olive," Malsumis says, walking over to give me a quick kiss before grabbing the garland for the staircase. "Come help me deck these halls."

Kap and I begin putting the lights on the tree as we hear laughter from the hall.

"I am not trying to pry, but you and Malsumis seem to be doing well. I was worried after everything that happened." Gluskap says.

"We are doing well. We have worked through so much together, and it has made us stronger."

"I am glad. I can only hope that he and I can continue to grow as we once were," he says, glancing toward the hall where Set and Malsumis continue to laugh and joke.

"You may not ever be like you once were, but you will be something new, something stronger," I reply.

"I hope you are right, Olive."

"I usually am," I laugh. That earns me a chuckle.

Gluskap goes to say something when his attention is drawn to a commotion behind me. He breaks out in laughter as I turn around to see Set with mistletoe hanging in the front of his pants. I roll my eyes and shake my head at him as he stands there grinning.
Malsumis is behind him, laughing and being of no help at all.

"I think I am going to wear this kissing plant tomorrow when your friends are here. That brown haired one is feisty." Set says.

"No, you're not going to wear that. Jennifer is her name, and stay away from her, and that kissing plant is going to leave a rash on your dick, so I would get it out of your pants."

Gluskap and Malsumis erupt into laughter while Set rushes to pull the mistletoe from his zipper.

"Gods damnit, Mal! Why did you let me put poison on my cock?" Set bellows before he goes off to the bathroom.

"When have I ever been able to stop you from doing something stupid? Besides, it is hilarious." Malsumis laughs as he joins Gluskap and me at the tree.

"I give you two one job," I tease.

"I made sure it was done, Love," he says as he leans in to kiss me.

"That is my cue to go," Gluskap says. "I will see you tomorrow for the festivities."

"Bye, Kap!"

"Goodbye, Brother," Malsumis says as he hugs Gluskap. They both smile at each other, and then Gluskap disappears.

"Good news, everyone, my cock is rash free!" Set announces as he enters the room.

"Surprising considering your…um…partners," Malsumis teases.

"Ew, and just when I was thinking about letting you join us for a Christmas threesome. Shoot," I joke.

"Gods Damnit, Mal! You and your big mouth!" Set explodes as we laugh. "That is it. I am leaving. You two are assholes, and I will see you tomorrow." Then he is gone.

"Do you think we should have told him that it was fake mistletoe?" I ask.

"Absolutely not. Did you see his face? That was great." Malsumis laughs.

"It is so good to see you happy. I am glad to have your brother and Set around to help with that."

"Olive, you are my happiness."

"You are mine, my Love."

Malsumis caresses the side of my face and brushes his lips against mine. I lean into his lips and deepen the kiss. He slides one of his hands to the back of my neck to pull me in closer, and the other goes around my waist. He moves his hands to the hem of my shirt, never breaking our kiss. He pulls off my top and begins feverishly unbuttoning and pushing down my jeans. I wiggle out of my pants, and he takes a step back. He stands there taking me in with a heat in his eyes I haven't seen in a long while.

"What is it?" I ask softly.

"I just want to admire what is mine. Go sit, Olive," he commands, his voice thick with want. My nipples harden at the thought of what comes next.

I do as he says as he begins removing his clothes. By the time he reaches me in the chair, he is completely nude. I am the one who gets to admire what is mine. Gods, he is beautiful. His raven black hair flows down his muscular back. I take in his perfect chest and well defined abs. He kneels before me and looks me in the eyes before taking my nipple into his mouth, sucking and letting it go with a pop. He begins circling my clit with his tongue before pushing two fingers in me. I lean my head back and moan.

"Look at me, my mate."

I look down at him, and he takes a long, languid lick.

"I want to watch you come undone, Olive."

Those words send shivers throughout my body. I do as he says and look into his onyx eyes as he goes down on me. He sucks on my clit as he hits the spot inside of me that he knows will send me over the edge. I am so close to coming, and his intense look is only sending me closer to that edge. When he starts eating me like I am his last meal, I come so hard I see stars. I scream out his name, and he doubles down on his efforts. My knees begin to shake, and I feel him smile against me.

"Ride me, Olive."

I stand on wobbly legs, and he sits in the chair. I straddle him as he pulls me down for a kiss with the taste of me still on his tongue.
I lift up and slowly lower myself onto his cock.

"My Olive," he moans quietly.

I pick up my rhythm, and he wraps his arms around me, bringing me in and burying his face into my neck, pushing and pulling me so I bounce harder on him. He moves his hands down to my hips and holds me so hard I am sure there will be bruises later. He begins to thrust, matching my movements.

"Fuck. Just. Like. That." He growls.

I can't take any more, and I begin to come again, throwing my head back and moaning out for him. He comes with me, roaring my name, then biting down hard on my neck, which only intensifies my orgasm. As we come down, he holds me close, kissing my neck and shoulder.

We stay this way by the fire for several long moments, enjoying the closeness that we so desperately have missed.

Chapter 43: Malsumis

"Do I have to wear this? It is hideous," I complain. I am wearing a red and green sweater with a tree on the front and fuzzy garland strung on it.

"Yes! It is an ugly Christmas sweater dinner," Olive explains. She has on a deep blue sweater covered in glitter felt stars and a lopsided moon. For some reason, there are five tiny stuffed sheep dangling from yarn, so they bounce when she walks. I would much rather watch her other assets bounce, but she said that would have to wait.

"I do not like this already, but I will endure it for you."

"My hero," she laughs.

I smile and lean in to kiss her. For her, I would endure anything thrown at me.

"Now I think I have everything ready for dinner!" she says excitedly. She insisted on cooking a big meal because that was what she and Mark did together, and it makes her feel close to him. I understand that, so I assist where I can.

"I am here!" Set announces from the other room.

"We are in the kitchen," Olive calls out. My back is to the door when he walks in, but Olive bursts out laughing. I turn to see Set in a bright red sweater, stitched with a blinking battery powered reindeer whose nose flashes like it is sending a distress signal.

There are tiny bells sewn into the fabric that jingle every time he thinks about moving.

"What the fuck are you wearing?" I ask, laughing.

"It is festive! You two do not know good tradition."

"Hello! Merry Christmas!" Gluskap exclaims, "Nice sweater, Set."

"See! At least someone knows good traditions!" Set says as he stomps out, jingling all the way to the couch.

"There is something I need to tell you, Malsumis," Gluskap starts.

"It is okay, Kap, I know I am the more handsome brother."

"Haha, but no. It is about Father. He wants to see you."

"Then he can come see me himself instead of using you as a go between."

"I planned on it, my son," my father's voice comes from behind me. Olive looks behind me and then back at me.

"Surprise, Brother," Glauskap says.

I turn around and see my father. He is dressed in mortal clothing for the first time that I have ever seen. He even looks festive in a simple red and green sweater.

"Hello, Malsumis, I have been calling for you, but it seems as though you have gotten good at ignoring me. Not that I blame you.

I have not been the best that I could have been for you, but I have always loved you, my son."

"Wow, that is a lot to come here and drop on him at once…what do I even call you?" Olive steps up to defend me. Not that I need her to, but I love to see her feisty.

"My name cannot be pronounced in modern language. You can call me Tala, though. I know my presence is a surprise and is much to be presented, but I do want to know my son. I will not stay if you two want me to go."

"Well, Tala…" Olive starts.

"It is okay, Love," I kiss her head and turn to my father. "You can stay." Everyone looks at me, shocked. I really am trying to change not only for Olive but for myself. I have held on to hurt and resentment for so long, I just want to be happy and content. I have the opportunity for that.

"Thank you, my son. I promise to be on my best behavior."

"You better," Olive adds sassily. Gods, I love her.

The doorbell ringing breaks the tension. Olive goes to greet Jennifer and Candy, leaving me alone with my family. From here in the kitchen, I can hear the jingling of Set's sweater.

"What is that incessant noise?" Father asks.

"Set," Gluskap and I laugh at the same time.

"I should have known it was Set," Father chuckled. Chuckled. I have never heard that noise come from him. Judging by the look on his face, neither has Glusksap.

"Why are the two of you looking at me like I have grown another head?" Father asks.

"Why are you acting like this?" I question.

"Like what?"

"Normal?" Gluskap adds.

"I am trying to connect with my sons. I have been reflecting. I have been so obsessed with right and wrong and the complete balance of things that I almost lost Malsumis. I know I cannot change the past or even have a perfect relationship, but I want to have some kind of connection with my sons. If you will have me."

"Of course, I will, Father," Gluskap says after a moment.

I look down for several moments. He has never been there for me emotionally. Do I accept him trying now? Do I deny him like he has all these years? That makes me no better than him if I do.

"I want to try," I say finally.

My father smiles at me for the first time that I can remember. Olive enters the kitchen and arches a brow.

"Is everything okay in here, or do I need to kick someone's ass?"

"No, my mate, no ass kicking is necessary," I laugh.

"Well, the girls and Set are starving, so let's eat!"

"How can I help?" Father asks.

Olive directs him to carry the ham to the table and then instructs Gluskap and me to take the sides. We all take our seats around the table. Olive sits beside me and is laughing at something that Jennifer said, and I slide my hand into hers. I look around at our family and friends and think to myself that, for once in my life, I am at peace and have a family.

Chapter 44: Mark

I begin walking away from the river, carrying the weight of what I just did with me. I had to choose. It was her or me. I couldn't just give up; I had to fight. I had to pick myself. I had to pick Olive. Right? The look of fear on the girl's face when she realized I wasn't going to save her replays over and over in my head as I travel aimlessly through Tartarus.

I don't know how long I have walked, but suddenly, there are three mirrors in a room in front of me. If my Greek mythology serves me correctly, these are the Mirrors of Destiny. The air thickens around me as I step further into the chamber where the mirrors are. This room feels like it has been carved from dread itself. Every breath gets harder to take, sending waves of gloom through my body. The chamber is dark, but even in the darkness, there are shadows moving. I move to stand in the center of the mirrors themselves. They are not actual mirrors in the sense that I can see my reflection in them. They rise from the ground like sheets of shimmering silver. The surfaces shiver, but not from any breeze, because there are none here, but more like they sense me watching them.

They watch back.

I start hearing faint whispers throughout the room. Not exactly clear voices, but like the memory of voices. They carry the weight of lingering regret and half formed possibilities. Tartarus is heavy; this is nearly unbearable. This is the heaviness of no mercy.

"Step closer, Marcus the Reforged," the Mirror directly in front of me breathes.

I obey.

My reflection forms in the center mirror, then splits to the other two. The reflection in front of me is myself right now, stronger and immortal yet tired, sad, angry, and stubbornly alive despite Tartarus's hunger.

The mirror to my left is a sharper version of myself. Taller, even stronger, and eyes full of power with the godly spark that has been forced on me.

The mirror to my right is the worst of the three. It is me if fear and sadness win. Hollow, unanchored by love, just a puppet for Tartarus's despair.

All three stand in the mirrors, three separate truths. The silver mirrors ripple outward, and the three versions step forward.

My breath catches. I feel every path tug at my spine.

My mortal self whispers of who I was before dying, before being thrown here, before being reborn.

My immortal self carries my destiny like a blade. Dangerous and frighteningly heavy with my new power.

My hollow self waits with hunger, offering a terrible surrender.

"Who will you choose to become?" the mirrors whisper together.

I stand here dumbfounded. I have to choose. Do I stay stagnant and never make it out? Do I change into something dangerous and someone I don't know? Do I do nothing and let the fear of choosing take over, and put my life in the hands of the mirrors' judgment?

I lift my shaking hand and begin to choose my fate.

The mirrors still.

The three reflections fade into shimmering silhouettes, awaiting my decision. The pressure is too much. Everything feels too heavy, like Tartarus itself is holding its breath waiting for me to choose.

Just as I reach my hand out, I think of Olive. I let the thought of her soft voice coax the terror from my bones. I imagine what it would be like to have her in my arms once again. I think of Mal. I think of his fierce devotion to Olive, and how he, in the end, tried to save me. I let them become my shelter.

My heart knows my answer before my mind does.

"I choose them."

The mirrors react instantly. Their surfaces begin to brighten, but not with cold silver. They turn into the warm color of dawn breaking. The chamber fills with whispers and a light swirling breeze. The three silhouettes merge into one in the center mirror. "You choose love over fear. You choose your connections over destiny's chains that are woven in your very being. You choose Dream and Chaos. You choose your own fate."

Searing pain brings me to my knees. My skull feels as though it is being split in two. I double over with a pain so intense I feel like I am going to be sick.

The pain starts to subside, and I feel a gentle, cool breeze brush my cheek, something impossible for Tartarus.

Then I feel them.

First, my girl. My sweet Olive.

A warmth blooms in my chest. I feel her presence like a whispered lullaby. I feel her sadness caused by my absence and how desperately she misses me. My heart shatters.

"Olive, I'm here! I will come back to you!"

Olive fades, and a pulse of wildfire ignites at my spine. A protective surge wraps around me. It is raw, fierce. Mal. I feel Mal.
How is this possible?

"Take care of our girl, Mal," I whisper.

I am finally able to stand and look in the mirror. I am the same, but there is something different in my presence. Something more powerful. Something not mortal, not god, but something new. A being shaped by primal forces.

The mirrors have accepted my choice. They fracture. They don't shatter, though; there is a crack large enough for me to enter through that leads deeper into Tartarus.

The portal stabilizes, and there is a whisper from Tartarus…
"You have chosen love in a place built on despair. Come forward and carry what is forbidden here."

I step through the crack and one step closer to Olive.

Chapter 45: Olive

"HAPPY HEARTS DAY!!!" Set yells from the bottom of the stairs.

"We really need to block him from entering this house," Malsumis says grumpily, as he pulls me closer to the bed.

"Hmm, that is tempting," I giggle. "We should probably put clothes on before he gets impatient and storms up here."

"I guess. I would hate to have to pluck his eyes from his eye for seeing you naked."

I try to get up, but I'm pulled back to the bed. Before I know it, Malsumis is on top of me.

"On second thought, let him wait," he says, kissing down my chest before rising to capture my mouth so I couldn't protest as if I would. My sexy mate…on top of me…yes please!

I wrap my legs around him, pulling him in closer to me. He looks down at me with his long hair falling around his face. I reach up and tuck one side behind his ear, and he leans into my hand, kissing it. He looks back down at me, taking me in. I feel his hard cock begin to grind against me as he looks at me intensely and says nothing. I'm naked, but with him looking at me like this makes me feel even more bare if that is even possible. He reaches down and pushes two of his fingers inside of me.

"Is this for me, Olive?"

"Yes," I pant as he increases his speed and pressure.

"Are you ready for me?"

"Yes…please…Malsumis."

He slides in me excruciatingly slow, until he is entirely inside of me. My head tilts back, and I let out a low moan. It begins to feel like he is touching me everywhere at once. I open my eyes and see his shadows skimming all over my body. I need more of him.

"More…Malsumis…harder."

He continues to watch me as he quickens his pace, his hands grabbing my hips hard, pulling me up so he can thrust harder. His shadows begin to circle my clit, and just when I think I can't take any more, I feel pressure from behind. My eyes widen, and he smirks. I am overwhelmed by the sudden fullness, but I don't stop him.

"Malsumis…I'm going to come…"

"That's it, come for me, Olive," he says in a deep, breathy voice.

I begin to see stars, like literal stars. As I come, the room fills with a swirl of darkness and silver lights. I call out his name as I clench around him. That has him chasing his own release. He pounds into me harder, sweat glistening off his abdomen. He growls my name as he comes.

He lies beside me, drawing lazy circles on my stomach, and suddenly the door bursts open.

"WAKE UP… Oh fuck yes…" Set starts, and he pushed out with the door slamming in his face. "Come on, Mal!!" Set calls from the hall.

"That is it. I am taking his eyes."

"Malsumis, we did keep him waiting. You know he has been excited about Valentine's Day."

"Why is he even excited? He does not have anyone."

"That isn't very nice," I chastise with a smirk. " He is our best friend. We told him we would have a Valentine's Day lunch with him."

"Fine. He can keep his eyes for today. After that, I promise nothing."

"I would expect nothing less, my Love," I say, leaning over for a kiss.

Just to make Set wait a little longer, Malsumis takes his time with me in the shower. When we go downstairs, Set is waiting.

"FINALLY! If you two are not going to let me join in, at least hurry up with your *lovemaking*," he says with annoyance, then he smirks. "By the way, Olive, you looked simply delicious," he laughs and takes off running toward the back door.

"YOU SON OF A BITCH!" Malsumis takes off after him.

Malsumis stops, and tendrils of black shadows reach for Set. They grab his ankles, and he goes down hard on the floor. A gold flair of light flies toward Malsumis, but he never falters; he continues to pull Set to him.

"I promised Olive I would not pluck your eyes from your head, but I did not say I would not kick your ass," Malsumis yells as he dives on top of Set.

The two of them are rolling on the floor fighting, Malsumis is clearly winning this fight.

"Well, if you two are going to waste your time on the floor together, I'm going to find someone else to take me on a lunch date," I say nonchalantly.

Malsumis throws one last punch and then is in front of me in seconds with a wild look in his eyes. He stalks me until I'm backed into the wall, he takes my face into his hands, and kisses me with an untamed passion.

"You are mine," he says into my lips when he breaks the kiss.

"I was just joking," I give a breathy laugh.

"Do not joke about something that would end me."

I pull him down into another kiss until Set clears his throat.

"Can we leave now that Mal is finished trying to kick my ass?"

"Trying? I absolutely was kicking your ass," Malsumis quips back.

"I was letting you," said Set.

"Do I need to prove it again?" Malsumis comes back.

"I can't believe you two would fight on Valentine's Day. The day of love. Shame on you both," I say with a laugh.

"Oh, you want love?" Malsumis says with a grin, putting his hands on my waist.

"Enough of that! I am tired of waiting on you two and your…*love*," Set whines. "Can we just go already?"

"Fine," Malsumis growls in annoyance.

We arrive at the little retro diner conveniently called Retro Diner, very original. When Set gets out of the car, I see that he has changed his shirt into a red sweater with pink hearts all over it.

"You look ridiculous," Malsumis says and rolls his eyes.

"You wound me, Mal. I will have you know that this is mortal fashion for this day. You, in your jeans and leather jacket, look ridiculous."

I have to disagree. Malsumis in jeans and a leather jacket looks far from ridiculous. If Set weren't here, we would be in the backseat of the car right now.

Malsumis and I walk into the diner, and it is decorated wall to wall with pink and red paper hearts hanging from the ceiling and an inflatable cupid that looks one good breeze from deflating.

Behind us, Set practically kicks in the door like he owns the place.

"Behold! The land of love and overpriced couples specials!" he says dramatically.

"Um…a table for three?" The hostess blinks and stumbles over her words.

"Yes, thank you," I say.

"Do not worry, Olive, we will witness one of my great loves…watching Set embarrass himself," Malsumis says quietly to me with a grin.

"I would never embarrass myself, only you, Mal," Set says sweetly.

Suddenly, Set gasps, and snatches a pair of novelty heart shaped glasses from the hostess stand, and puts them on. They are pink.

They are glittery. They look absurd. They are so Set.

"See? I'm not embarrassed!"

We roll our eyes as the hostess walks us to our booth. I slide into one side, and Malsumis sits beside me and begins drumming his fingers on the table. Set plops down into the other side of the booth and immediately starts messing with the centerpiece. "Thank you for celebrating Love Day with me. I know you would rather be somewhere alone, but this does mean a lot to me," Set says with raw honesty.

"Aw, Set! You're welcome! You are our best friend, of course, we want to show you that you are loved!" I say. "Well, if you really want to show me how much…"

"Set…" Malsumis growls.

"It was just a suggestion," Set says, raising his hands in surrender.

The waiter walks up, and Malsumis immediately puts his arm around my shoulder. As if I would even entertain the idea of being with anyone else other than him or…Mark. It's been eight months since he has been gone, and the ache is still there. Malsumis senses my thoughts, pulls me in, and kisses my head. I look up and smile at him.

"Can I get you anything to drink?" the waiter asks.

"Bring me your most romantic beverage, sir. Something that screams love," Set explains to the waiter.

"I will have the strawberry lemonade," I answer.

"Coffee. Black," Malsumis says.

The waiter nods and walks away.

"Ugh, Mal, could you pick a less romantic drink?" Set complains.

Malsumis just shrugs and smirks. Set turns and looks at the pitiful cupid inflatable and suddenly deflates with a pitiful wheeze and conveniently lands on Malsumis's head. Set erupts in laughter, and I grab my phone and snap a picture.

"Set, I am going to kill you," Malsumis says with a laugh, removing the cupid from his head.

"Best Valentine's Day EVER," Set cackles.

For the rest of lunch, we eat, we joke, we bicker. Even in all the absurdity, we look like the happiest little family.

Chapter 46: Malsumis

I sensed Olive was sad at lunch, and I know it was because she misses Mark. At one point, that would have hurt me deeply, but I understand it now. I feel the connection with him. Not as strongly as the two of them had, but it is still there.

We planned to order in dinner this evening, but I thought that it would be better to cook together. It will be fun, plus she used to cook with Mark, so this may help her feel connected to him, too. However, I may have overestimated my kitchen skills.

We are in the kitchen, and I am trying to take the lead, but this cookbook is staring back at me like it wants to attack me. The pot on the stove simmers, miraculously, not boiling over.

"Okay…pasta should not explode. Probably," I mutter to myself.

I glance over at Olive, and in that moment, all the wildness inside of me softens. She does that to me. Calms my storm. She makes me almost…shy.

"I am trying," I say, half in defense, half hopeful. "I wanted to make tonight…calm and special for you."

She slips behind me at the stove and wraps her arms around my waist.

"You don't have to tame your chaos, she says quietly. "I love you exactly as you are."

The kitchen smells like garlic, butter, and something that I was not supposed to burn, but in just that single touch, I am relaxed.

She stirs the pot as I sprinkle in seasonings. She laughs when I insist I meant to put in half the jar.

"I can fix this," I say, pointing at the skillet. It erupts in flames.

The smoke alarm goes off. I erupt in a barrage of curse words that I am positive Olive has never heard before. Olive laughs until she cries while she stands back and watches.

"I will just order pizza," I laugh.

"Oh no, you won't!" Olive says. "You worked hard on this. The pasta and salad are perfectly edible, so we will eat your dinner."

"I cannot guarantee the safety of this meal."

"Oh, don't overreact, it's fine, come on, let's take it to the table."

Dinner may be a disaster.

It might be perfect.

Either way, the evening is exactly what I hoped it would be. Just the two of us together, calm shaped from chaos.

We get all the food set on the table, and I light candles around the room. We sit beside each other and begin to eat.

"Mmm. Not bad for the cooking disaster of the century," I say.

"It wasn't that bad, my Love. You just get stressed out."

"Me? Stressed? No, not possible. I am a calming presence," I gasp dramatically.

"That is the funniest thing I have heard all day, and we spent the afternoon with Set!"

"You love me anyway," I say with a grin.

"The jury is still out," she teases, as she pretends to be considering it by tapping her chin.

"Then let me persuade the jury," I say, moving in closer.

"With bribery?"

"Obviously," I say into her ear.

My hand slides up her thigh. Oh, naughty Olive, no panties. She stills as I begin rubbing her clit. She spreads her legs wider for me, never taking her eyes off me. She is so wet already. I stop, and she gives a pouty whine. I smirk and give her my hand.

"Stand, my Olive."

She does as I say, and I clear the table of the food. I will clean it up later. Right now, I want to eat something far better. I sit her on the table, and the realization of what is happening hits her. She slides her dress off over her head. I will never get tired of looking at my goddess. She is perfection.

I sit at the head of the table and grab her legs, pulling her to the edge. I place my hands on both thighs and spread her legs apart, and I start kissing her down her inner thigh, sucking lightly when I get near her pussy. I lick her slowly all the way up to her clit, and that elicits a low moan from her. I continue to tease her. I flatten my tongue and increase my efforts, and am rewarded with the prettiest breathy sounds from my Olive. I take her clit between my lips and begin licking it steadily. That has her grabbing my hair and arching her back. I push two of my fingers into her and continue licking her.

"Malsumis…don't stop…Mal…" she calls out.

Within seconds, she lets out loud moans, and her legs begin to shake. I stand, continuing to finger her. She is so beautiful as she comes undone on me. I pull my fingers out of her and begin removing my clothing. She leans up on her elbows to watch me, eyes full of want and desire. I start stroking myself as she watches, and she goes to come to me.

"Stay there, Olive."

I take hold of her legs and put her feet on my shoulders and push my cock into her warm, wet pussy. She feels like my own personal heaven. At this angle, I can get much deeper than usual, and she feels divine.

"I am going to fuck you, Olive. Are you ready for that?"

"Yes…Gods yes," she breathes.

"I am the only god you will call out to, Olive," I growl as I thrust into her hard.

"Malsumis!" she cries out.

"That's right, love."

I steady my pace to enjoy her beautiful body lying out before me. I cannot take it anymore, and I begin to chase my own release. As I do, Olive slips a hand between us and starts fingering herself. It only feeds my want for her. She reaches her climax just before I do, and the feeling of her clenching my cock sends me over the edge. Both of us are panting and breathless.

"You have persuaded the jury," she says, and we both laugh.

After we shower and clean up from dinner, we lie on the couch together and turn on a movie. With Olive in my arms, everything feels right. She is mid laugh at something that was said on screen when she suddenly stops. Then I feel it too.

A pulse.

Not a sound. Not a light. Something deeper. The unmistakable imprint of a soul brushing ours.

Olive's breath catches, and her eyes widen.

I sit up and look at her.

"What was that?" she asks.

"It felt like…Mark." I murmur. " But not like he was before. He feels different. Stronger. Clearer."

"It felt like he was reaching for us."

"What is happening to him?" I ask aloud to no one in particular.

Before we can say anything, we both sense something else.

A strong pulse.

Sharp. Wrong.

Mark's presence is cut off.

Abruptly. Violently.

Olive gasps and falls back on the couch as if a string inside of her snapped.

I snarl and clutch the armrest of the couch.

"He's in pain," Olive says, voice trembling. "Something grabbed him."

"Tartarus took him back," I say with white hot fury.

Chapter 47: Mark

I walk toward the portal, thinking I will be walking one step closer to my girl and Malsumis. That is not what happens. As I walk up to the portal, it flickers and then collapses like a dying star. The golden crack slams shut, and Tartarus swallows any light.

The floor beneath me opens, and I am yanked downward.

I am hit with an inferno of heat that burns my lungs just by breathing. I try screaming, but I can't.

I am slammed into a cell carved of living flames.

The walls are not solid. They are pillars of burning light twisted into bars. Each flame rises taller than any man. Flickering in between them, I can see others around me. I see faces, claws, and shadows of those trapped here like me.

"You chose love. Tartarus chooses punishment," voices whisper to me.

The floor is scorching but doesn't burn me. Tartarus doesn't want me dead just to suffer.

From above, I hear Olive's voice like a fading dream. I feel Mal's fury roaring like distant thunder. They felt me. They know I am here, that I haven't given up.

I reach my hand toward them, and the flames rise higher and higher, sealing me inside the cell. This cage was built for someone dangerous. That obviously isn't me. I mean, yes, I have powers and am an immortal now, but I am not dangerous. Am I?

I whisper their names.

"Olive…Mal."

For the first time since entering Tartarus, I am truly afraid.

Chapter 48: Olive

"What do you mean you felt him? He was mortal. He wasn't strong enough to do something like that from Tartarus. Not even the Titans trapped there can do that," Gluskap says, surprised.

"That is my boy. He is stronger than you think, Kap," Set says.

"We can't just ignore this as a fluke. We need to speak with someone who has better connections with Hades," Malsumis says.

"I will speak with Anubis and see if he has any ideas," Set says, and he is gone.

"I think we should speak with Father," Gluskap offers.

"I actually agree with you, brother," Malsumis says as he holds my hand.

We arrive in Tala's realm, and there are the soft hues of morning over the lands. Everything is shimmering in the breaking light. I would love to take in its beauty, but I want to get Mark back more. We knock on Tala's door, and a very disheveled and half naked, red haired woman answers.

"Can I help you?" She asks with annoyance.

"Where is our father?" Malsumis demands as he storms past her.

"Come in, please," the woman says sarcastically.

Gluskap and I walk in and find Malsumis standing in the hall laughing. We walk over, look in the bedroom, and see a very naked Tala tied to his bedposts.

"GET OUT!" Tala yells.

"Oh, for gods' sake, get out of here and let us get decent!" the red haired woman scolds.

We walk outside, all of us shocked by what we just saw.

"Father…has…a girlfriend…" Gluskap manages to get out between his laughter.

"I never thought I would see the day, and I definitely wish I had not seen that," Malsumis jokes.

"You guys don't kink shame him," I say, and we all begin laughing again.

"Haha, yes, laugh it up, you three," Tala says from behind us.

We turn to see him shirtless, but at least he's wearing pants. His long black hair, streaked with silver, flows freely. I have never seen him so…relaxed.

"So are you going to tell us who she is, or do we need to make this more awkward?" Malsumis asks. Tala releases an annoyed breath.

"Her name is Anastasia. She is a phoenix. She lives here with me now. Okay."

"I thought a phoenix was a bird," I say.

"A mortal misconception," Anastasia says as she walks up beside Tala.

"What can I help you three with?" Tala asks as he takes Anastasia's hand in his.

"We felt Mark reaching out to us, then Tartarus pulled him in," I explain.

"That's impossible. Unless…no, Hades would never allow it," Tala starts.

"What?" Gluskap asks.

"Unless he has become something else. Something that Tartarus fears getting stronger."

"He felt stronger when he reached for us," Malsumis adds.

"We can try to open a pathway to Tartarus, but I must warn you, the Mark you pull out will not be the Mark you knew," Tala explains.

"What do you mean?" I ask.

"Mortals who enter Tartarus do not return. Ever. You may be able to pull him out, but he will not be whole."

"He went to Tartarus because of me. I will get him back. Whole. He does not deserve the torment that he is enduring." Malsumis says.

Tala studies us for a long moment and looks down at Anastasia. She nods.

"We will open a narrow path, one that Tartarus will not notice at first. Understand that he has to choose to rise into what he has become and what he is becoming." Tala says.

"We will make him choose life. We will remind him that he is not alone, like he did for me." Malsumis says, voice low.

"We will bring him home," I say and look up at Malsumis. He kisses my head.

"Go together, but remember Tartarus listens," Tala says.

Malsumis takes my hand, and I squeeze his.

Tala raises his hand, and a rift of light forms. It opens to show flames and deep shadow, and then snaps closed. He tries again. Again. Again. He looks at us with regret carved in his features.

"I cannot."

Malsumis stiffens beside me, and I hold my breath.

"Tartarus has sealed itself shut," Anastasia says, quietly, just as shocked as we are.

"Sealed, against *us*?" Malsumis asks, shadows gathering at his feet.

"Against anyone who would interfere. Mark's presence has awakened old powers. Tartarus mistakes him for a threat," Tala informs us.

"He will die there," I cry.

"My dear, he is already dead. He is something different now." Anastasia says.

"What is he?" Malsumis asks.

"We do not know, son. Something new. Something powerful enough for Tartarus to fear." Tala answers.

"Then what are we supposed to do? Stand here while he burns?" Malsumis snarls.

"We cannot create a path to him, but he can create one to you," Anastasia says.

Silence drops like a blade.

"He has to break through Tartarus from the inside," I say, full of terror.

"Yes. Only a rising power can fracture the walls imprisoning him. Only his will can get him out." Tala explains.

"He has been fighting for so long. He has been clawing through for eight months. How much more can he…" Malsumis's voice breaks. "How much more can he take?"

"Enough…if he remembers why he fights," Tala says gently.

Chapter 49: Mark

The flame cell pulses around me like a living heartbeat. One that doesn't match my own. Every time I push against the fiery bars, they coil up my arms with cruel intelligence, wrapping heat around me until the pain is just too much for me to take, and I let go.

I back away, breathing hard.

"Come on…come on…" I repeat, my voice cracking.

I throw myself at the bars, trying brute force. They explode outward, hurling me and skidding through the cell. I hit the ground through sparks that sting like needles. I cough and my eyes water from the smoke. I try again. And again. And again.

 Every time has the same result. Thrown. Burned. Bruised. Defeated.

"You cannot escape. You were meant to break." Tartarus whispers.

I try to stand, my legs shaking. My palms are blistered. My breath is ragged. I attempt a hundred more times, maybe more.

Time means nothing here, only suffering. I lean my head against the burning bars, welcoming the sting because it reminds me that I am still someone.

I try to scream in anger, but my voice collapses into a hoarse whisper. I sink to my knees, shoulders slumping. I stay like this for so long that my legs refuse to move when I try to stand. I curl into a ball on the floor. I want to go home to Olive, build a relationship with Mal, and get out of here. It is impossible, though. For a moment, I let the intrusive thoughts win. I give up. I let the flames close in. I let Tartarus claim me. I let the weight of destiny smother what's left of me.

"I can't...I can't do this anymore."

The flames dim, leaning in like predators to their prey.

"Yes, break," Tartarus purrs.

Something in me cracks. Not like breaking, more like opening. A memory of the Mirrors of Destiny asking me who I chose to become.

I had chosen them.

I had chosen love.

I had chosen myself.

A spark ignites deep in my soul. It's not mortal. It's not godly. It is something that only exists because I do. Something new.

The flames around me recoil like they are startled.

Golden light begins to bleed from beneath my skin, starting at my heart. My eyes snap open, seeing everything clearer than they ever have.

I rise slowly and lift a hand. No force. No shouting. No brute strength. Just will, the same will that chose love in a place built to devour it.

A golden light lashes out from my hand and wraps around the bars. The flames fear me as they melt away, screaming. They are shattered or forced open. They are unmade.

The cell collapses.

Tartarus roars, furious and shaking violently. A deep, ancient rumble vibrates through the realm. I stand in the center, glowing and alive.

"I am not yours."

I step forward through the parting flames. All eyes from the neighboring cells are on me. Some in fear, some in respect of the one that Tartarus cannot hold.

Chapter 50: Malsumis

It has been three months since we last felt Mark, 11 months since Zeus killed him. We have been trying to find a way to reach him every day, with no luck. Set and Gluskap have been helping to search for a way to break through Tartarus's forces, but have come up with nothing as well. I refuse to give up. Mark did not give up on me even when I gave him no reason to try. I will not give up on him now.

Olive is standing on the back deck, looking out at the still sleeping world. I walk up and wrap her in my arms, and she leans back into me.

"Nothing?" I ask, knowing the answer.

"No. He is just gone. When I call out, Tartarus just swallows the sound," her voice trembles.

"I hate feeling powerless," I snarl.

"I do too."

I begin pacing and drag my hand through the front of my hair.

"If I could rip that prison apart, I would. If I could even tear a hole big enough to pull him through, I would," I say angrily.

"Father said Tartartus feared him, that he was something different. New. What is he now? What if he isn't himself anymore?"

"I have had the same thought," Olive admits, with unshed tears in her eyes.

I gather her in my arms and just hold her. Honestly, I do not know what to do. I hate this helpless feeling. I want to protect her, but I cannot, not against this pain. I need to do something for her.

Something to ease the weight of all these months. Hell, maybe I need it for myself too.

Later in the afternoon, I call Set and Gluskap to come and keep Olive distracted. We start a movie, and I slip out while Olive dozes off.

When I return, I am met with a furious Olive. She marches up to me and points her finger at my chest.

"Where did you go? I couldn't find you anywhere! I was so worried! These two knuckleheads wouldn't tell me what was going on!"

"Hey! I'm offended!" Set gasps. He turns to Gluskap. "What is a knucklehead?" Gluskap just shrugs.

"I am sorry, my Olive. I have a surprise for you. I did not mean to worry you, but I need you to get dressed to go out on a date." I say calmly and kiss her head.

"Really? You planned a random date for me?" she asks, her anger subsiding.

I nod and smile. She leans up for a kiss, and I am more than happy to oblige.

"I will go and get ready!" She says as she runs to the stairs.

"Thanks for keeping her distracted and calm, you two knuckleheads," I say, turning to Set and Gluskap.

"We tried! Have you ever told her to calm down? She only got more furious, and we did not know what to do!" Gluskap exclaims.

"What is a knucklehead?" Set asks exhaustedly.

"Dumbass. It means you are a dumbass," Olive says from behind me.

I turn to see her in a form fitted purple dress that shows her curves perfectly. On second thought, we may not leave this house tonight.

"Damn girl," Set says.

"I second that," Gluskap adds.

Before I can turn around, they both laugh and disappear.

"See, dumbasses," Olive laughs.

"You look like I want to keep you to myself tonight, my Love."

"We could stay home if you would rather do that."

"No, I have something special for you planned." I take her hand and take her to an alley lit with string lights between the old brick buildings.

I lead her down the alleyway, nervous that she will not like our date. We come to a tiny cafe called Luna & Lattes. I open the door for her and put my hand on the small of her back.

The cafe smells of warm vanilla and cinnamon. I paid for the cafe to stay open after hours just for us, and there are no other customers here. I guide her to our booth, which is decorated with a moon motif. She looks at me, and I smirk faintly.

"They usually are not open this late," she says.

"I paid them to stay open."

"You mean you talked to people?"

"Hey, I can be very civilized," I say, pretending to be offended.

She laughed, a soft sound I have not heard in months. My chest cracks open in relief. "You're trying to distract me." I do not try to deny it.

"You deserve a break from the pain," I say quietly.

The waiter brings our drinks that I preordered. Olive's cup is filled with a shimmering lavender latte dusted with edible glitter that looks like starlight.

"You remembered I like this one," she sounds surprised.

"I remember everything about you," I say.

She smiles and blows on her drink. I watch her like she is performing divine magic, which she is.

"Malsumis, you're staring."

"Am I?" I reply, absolutely staring.

"Yes," she takes a sip. "Stop," she says playfully.

"No," I lean my chin on my hand. "You are pretty."

"Malsumis…"

"What? I am distracting you and telling the truth."

"There is a difference between distraction and emotional ambush," she jokes.

"Are you accusing me of being emotionally competent?" I gasp dramatically.

"No, I am accusing you of being sweet on purpose."

"Do not spread rumors like that. I have a reputation to uphold." I tease.

"Of being a disaster?" she offered.

"A majestic disaster, thank you."

"You're impossible, my Warrior."

"You like me impossible."

"Only because someone has to keep you from causing a catastrophe," she quips, rolling her eyes.

"I will have you know I have not caused any catastrophes in…" I look down at my wrist at a pretend watch. "Two hours.

I will also have you know that if you roll your eyes at me again, you will pay for it later."

"Oh, will I?" She says…rolling her eyes.

"Tsk tsk, my Olive."

We finish our drinks and leave the cafe. We step out into an unseasonably warm night, the street glowing with warm lights. Olive suddenly stops walking.

"What's wrong, Love?"

"You said I would pay for rolling my eyes. I want my punishment now. Right now."

"Really? Okay, we will go home…"

"No," she interrupts. "Here in this alley, now."

"What? Here? What if someone sees us?" I am caught off guard.

"That's part of the excitement. If you aren't comfortable, though, we absolutely won't do it."

"No, no. I am in." I grab her and pull her behind a stack of wooden pallets.

I cradle her face in my hands and kiss her with a fire that has been building all night. This kiss is demanding. She matches my ferocity. As we kiss, her hands begin working feverishly at getting my jeans unfastened and pulled down. She breaks the kiss.

"No underwear, my naughty warrior," she says as she sinks to her knees. I gather her hair in my hand and pull it back. She begins kissing the underside of my cock with her wet lips. I have never felt anything more sensual. I almost come from that and the thrill of being out in the open. She takes me in her mouth and strokes me, and my base twisting her hand as she does. I she looks up at me from he position.

"You are so beautiful…fuck, you feel so good, Love."

She doubles down on her efforts as I thrust into her mouth. She is able to take me deep into her throat, and fuck me, she feels amazing. I can't take any more. I need to be in her now. I pull up on her hair, and she stands. I turn her around and pull up the hem of her short, fitted dress. She is so wet already. I push into her, and she gives me a low, breathy moan.

"Quiet, Love, or you will get us caught."

I increase my pace until the only sounds in the alley are the sound of our skin making contact and low, heavy breaths.

Seeing her bent over, holding on to the wooden pallets in an empty alley, is nearly sending me over the edge. When she begins to lose control and clamps her hand over her mouth to keep from making a sound, my movements become more erratic. I grab her hair and pull her head back. I have to fight the urge to call out her name as I come hard. Before I even pull out of her, we hear a voice. "Is someone out here?"

Olive giggles.

I get us the hell out of there.

Chapter 51: Mark

The moment that the cell collapses into molten sparks, Tartarus reacts like a wounded animal. The ground splits open, and a giant creature begins to crawl out from the fissure. The temperature drops and the flames dim and shrink back, as if they know what is about to happen.

This must be a guardian of the prison. Its body is a knot of limbs made of stone and bone. Its eyes are pits of smoke and ash. Every breath it takes sounds like rock grinding together. This thing towers over me at least three times my height.

The guardian tilts its head and speaks in a deep, sickening voice.

"Back to your cell."

I square my shoulders, my skin still glowing faintly gold. I am exhausted. I am aching everywhere, but I refuse to kneel for anyone again. Definitely not for Tartarus. Definitely not for this guardian.

The guardian moves first. It swings its massive hand down at me with the force of a collapsing building. I throw myself aside, and it narrowly misses me. It leaves a crater where I once stood.

I scramble up barely, and the guardian lunges again, swiping with its other arm. Sparks fly as its claws carve lines across the stone ground.

"Run, Markus," Tartarus whispers. "Hide. Break."

I don't. I refuse. I have made my choice, and I will never give up.

For the first time in my existence, I step toward the opposition, toward the danger.

The guardian roars and charges at me. Instinct tells me to dodge. Fear tells me to submit. But something deeper whispers to me.

"Stand your ground, Markus the Reforged."

I plant my feet. The creature's massive fist comes down. A power surges through me. It is new and foreign. Golden light bursts from my chest, wrapping my arms in threads of shimmering energy. It's not fire or lightning. It is like something that was already within me, sharpened. I lift my hands to the beast. It hits me full force. It stops. Frozen mid crush. I dig my heels into the ground, my muscles tremble under the weight, but I don't break. I am able to hold back a monster that could easily pulverize stone.

The guardian snarls in confusion and pushes harder.

I push back.

My golden energy surges up my arms and sparks across the guardian's limb. Cracks form instantly and glow like lava in the guardian's stone flesh. The creature jerks away, howling.

I barely have time to breathe before the creature slams a foot forward, sending a shockwave through the chamber. The force of it throws me against a wall. Pain bursts through my ribs. I cough and force myself up. I will not give Tartarus the satisfaction.

I raise a hand, and the golden thread forms again, winding around my fingers.

"Not this time," I growl.

The guardian charges again. Instead of dodging, I meet it head on. I thrust my glowing hand forward, and the thread lashes out. It stretches out into a glowing whip and wraps around the guardian's arm, burning into it.

The guardian tries to pull back, but I yank first. The enormous creature stumbles forward toward me. I swing the thread like a blade, slicing into the creature's stone core. The guardian howls out in panic and pain.

I step forward, my power stronger with every step. It isn't wild or chaotic. It is a steady, focused, determined power. My own power.

I channel everything into one strike. My pain. My will. My love for Olive. My want for Mal. The thread of light condenses into a bright golden spear.

I drive it straight into the creature's chest.

The guardian convulses, and cracks form all over its body. Seconds later, it collapses into crumbling stone and ash.

Silence follows.

It is like Tartarus shudders, realizing it underestimated me. I stand alone in the wreckage, breathing hard but unbroken.

"Try caging me again, mother fuckers." I mutter under my breath.

Chapter 52: Mark

I begin walking through Tartarus again. It is different this time. The fires dim as I walk by. Voices and whispers of the other prisoners are hushed as I pass.

I reach a point where ash is falling like snow. Everything is quiet beyond this point. I feel a strong power. A god is here. Hades. God of the Underworld.

I come up on a large gate carved from obsidian and bone. The gates opened as if in recognition. I hear whispers as I walk in. "He does not belong to death anymore."

Fucking right I don't.

I walk through a dark hall, and I see, who I assume is, Hades, on his throne. He sits straight, composed, almost statuesque. He is regal in his midnight robes that pool at his feet, and catch the glimmers of the firelight. His skin is light, his eyes are the color of ash, flecked with red embers. His hair lies in dark waves to his shoulders. Beside his thrones of stone and skulls is a more feminine one, carved from stone, with flowers carved into it.
Persephone's throne.

"You are not one of mine. Yet you walk through Tartarus as though it were your birthright," Hades says.

"I was sent here by Zeus's hand. Killed as payment for Eris's death."

"Then you should be ash and echo. Yet here you stand."

I stand tall beneath the weight of Hades's gaze. The tattoos of the chains from the Fates glow faintly up my arms and across my chest.

"I crossed the River Acheron, faced the Mirrors of Destiny, broke out of a cell built for a Titan, and fought a guardian. If death will not take me, then I will make meaning of what is left. Let me go, Hades."

"Meaning," Hades said thoughtfully. "Few immortals remember that word."

Hades rises from his throne, not out of anger, but more out of curiosity.

"Zeus demands balance through blood. He killed a mortal to pay for the death of a goddess. He is an idiot. Balance cannot be forced. It must become." Hades says as he studies my tattoos.

"The Fates never intervene against Zeus. You are special, Markus the Reforged." Hades extends his hand, tattooed and regal. "Walk free of this place, Markus. You owe me no death, but I grant you passage and a truth. Even gods fear what they cannot unmake. Make sure Zeus knows this."

I take his hand, and the underworld itself shifts. It feels as if Tartarus is exhaling, relieved that I am leaving. The gates open once more, and I begin my ascent out of Tartarus, closer to my girl.

First, I have to make a stop.

Chapter 53: Olive

It's been a year since Mark was killed. One year without him here. One year with him being trapped in Tartarus.

I snuggle into Malsumis, and he instinctively pulls me in closer to him.

"Olive…are you awake?" he whispers.

"Yes," I say, afraid to move, for fear the day will really start.

"Are you okay?"

"No. Can we stay in bed all day and skip this day?

"Absolutely."

"You can sleep," I say to him.

"If I sleep, I see him," he says, shaking his head.

"Me too." My chest tightens, and my eyes begin to tear.

"I am sorry I failed you both. I should have torn Tartarus apart before he ever reached it."

"It's not your fault, Malsumis. You could not have known that Zeus would throw him down there. We have both done everything we could."

He leans down and kisses me softly, then lies back and stares at the ceiling for several moments.

"We need a distraction," he says finally.

"What are you thinking?"

"It's a surprise. Get dressed in something comfortable."

Malsumis plugs the location into my phone, and I drive us there.

"LazerFunZone?" I say.

"Yes, it seems like just the distraction we need."

He is so proud of himself that I don't tell him that Mark and I played laser tag on one of our first outings together. Honestly, this makes me feel connected to Mark and Malsumis.

We walk inside to find a glow in the dark laser tag arena full of screaming children. There are adults, too, but the kids definitely outnumber them.

"No," I say.

"Olive, we must."

"If you hurt a single child…"

"I won't! I will be so gentle, like a destructive breeze," he says excitedly. "Really want us to play."

"Fine, but please be careful around any children."

Malsumis immediately starts dodging shots so fast I can barely see him. The children scream in delight.

"No powers," I hiss.

"I am using mortal ones. They are just…enhanced!"

He gets caught in a corner by a group of what looks to be eight year olds who ambushed him mercilessly. I watch him flail dramatically, then laugh. An actual laugh. A smile spreads across my face.

"Olive…they are monsters."

"They are children," I laugh.

"They have no mercy."

"You love it."

"Yes. Their violence is pure and ruthless," he laughs.

I am still laughing when one of the children runs up to me and pulls on my sleeve.

"Is your boyfriend okay?"

"He is my husband, and he is fine. Just dramatic."

The smile on Malsumis's face when I call him my husband is contagious. The kid nods at Malsumis and then shoots him again and runs off.

Once we were outside, Malsumis stretches like he has just been in battle.

"This was fun," I say.

"Fun? Tiny mortals nearly defeated me!"

"From where I was standing, you were defeated."

"Never repeat that," he laughs.

"You're laughing," I comment.

"You have been too."

"Thank you for today."

He wraps his arm around me, pulling me into him, and kisses me gently.

"EWW," one of the children from inside, leaving with his parent, says as he walks by.

Malsumis and I laugh.

"You will make the most amazing father one day," I say as I look up at him.

"Do you really think so? I must admit I have worried that I would not be good enough."

"Listen to me, you are enough. You are enough for me. You are enough for any children we have. You. Are. Enough." I say, taking his face in my hands.

"I love you, Olive," he says softly and bends down to kiss me.

We make it home after making a stop at Luna and Lattes for some coffee, only coffee this time, though. As soon as we walk into the house, Set and Gluskap are there.

"Where have you been? We have been calling all morning for you!" Set says quickly.

"Calm down, we just went out to get our minds off of what this month is," I say.

"Oh, that is right, it is June. Curious," Gluskap comments, looking at Set.

"Is someone going to tell us why you are here?" Malsumis interjects impatiently, looking at Gluskap.

"Tartarus is open again."

Chapter 54: Mark

Mount Olympus. Zeus's domain.

Thunder rolls across the heavens, and the air is split with lightning, but this time the storm answers to me, not Zeus.

Before me, the great hall of Olympus shimmers in the storm that has accompanied me. Pillars of marble pulse with faint light, and the air is thick with the power of the gods that are gathered here.

The doors groan as I push them open with a deliberately slow weight. All conversations fade into a hush as I step through the threshold with a power that wasn't borrowed from divinity but forced on me in ways that felt older, more profound, and hungrier than these gods have ever bothered to understand.

A ripple of discomfort passed across the hall as I approached Zeus slowly. Zeus has the fucking audacity to smirk at me. He thinks this is going to go his way.

"You dare come here, mortal? I cast you to Tartarus as payment for Eris's death!" Zeus's voice cracks the sky.

"Yet here I stand. Not mortal, not dead. You sought balance through destruction. Now you can no longer silence me."

"You reek of the underworld's touch," Hera says, leaning forward.

"Perhaps it is time that Olympus remembers what is beneath it, hmm?"

"You come to us, you dare to speak to us. Maybe it is time to remind you who I am, boy. Kneel," Zeus commands.

I laugh.

Not mockingly. Not loudly. Just a single breath of amusement.

All eyes are on me and Zeus and his red, angry face. Good.

I unfurl my power.

Shadows curl behind me like wings, and the air in the hall thickens with fear and uncertainty. The floor beneath Zeus cracks, just a small fracture, but enough to give a warning of who he was now dealing with. Zeus stumbles.

The so called King of Gods stumbles.

The entire pantheon inhales sharply.

"I don't kneel."

Zeus opens his mouth to speak, but the words die as soon as I make a step forward. His lightning arches backward. Recoiling from my presence. Fuck I wish Set could see this. He would love this shit.

In the silence between us, every god present is realizing something that they never expected to see.

Zeus is afraid.

He is trying to hide it. He straightens. He sets his jaw. When he grips his scepter, which he calls Lightning Bolt gods, this guy is a douche, his knuckles turn white, and he shifts a half step back. An instinctive retreat no one has ever seen from him.

I soften my expression, but not kindly.

"Don't worry if I wanted revenge, I wouldn't be standing here talking."

Zeus swallows.

The tension in the hall curls tighter. Oh, Zeus, don't try anything stupid. He is rattled but unwilling to lose face in front of his court. He lifts his arm. Lightning explodes from his palm, a streak of white, hot divine authority meant to remind me and everyone who is in charge here.

Surprise, Zeus…it's not you.

Gasps break out as the bolt roars straight for me.

I don't flinch.

I don't move.

I simply lift my hand.

The lightning stops mid air.

I fold the jagged body of the bolt in my palm as though it has always belonged there. The light wraps around my fingers, wild and erratic, but it does not burn me. I squeeze, and the lightning goes silent.

A shiver ripples through the hall. Shock, awe, disbelief. Zeus stares, thunder dying around him, like his power is ashamed of his failure.

"That," I say lazily, with the still swirling in my fingers, "was a mistake."

Zeus backs up a small step. Enough though. A murmur rose from the other gods.

I stopped short of his throne. Close enough that he has to tilt his chin up to maintain eye contact.

"You will never raise a hand or send anyone else to rise against me. You will never interfere with anyone I love or any soul tied to mine in any way."

"You dare to command…" Zeus starts, pride warring with fear.

I press my hand forward, and Zeus's own lightning leaped from my hand and hovered an inch from his throat. Not touching, but close enough that it is singeing his beard.

"Vow. It." I bite.

Zeus swallows, throat tight.

"I vow it," his voice wavers. There is no authority, he says, with the strain and brittle edge of someone who understands they are outmatched.

The lightning fizzles out instantly, and I let my arm fall to my side. He made a vow before all of Olympus, and it is unbreakable.

Zeus knows it.

I turn and walk out of the hall. The gods part for me. None speak. None breathe loudly. All that can be heard are my footsteps.

Today, I forced Zeus, King of Olympus, to bow without ever touching his knees.

Chapter 55: Malsumis

"What do you mean it is open?" Olive asks.

"Father and Anastasia have been trying every day to find a path to Mark. Then today one opened. They thought it might be a fluke, so they kept trying over and over. It is no fluke. Whatever closed Tartarus is gone." Gluskap explains.

"Are you two ready to go get our boy?" Set asks.

"Let go," I say, looking down at Olive.

We all travel to Father's realm, and he and Anastasia are both waiting for us. Dressed. Thank gods.

"Son, Olive," Father greets us both with an embrace. That is new.

"Kap and Set say you found a way into Tartarus?" Olive asks nervously, afraid this isn't real.

"Kap? I like that," Father chuckles. "Yes, whatever had Tartarus locked down is gone. We are now able to get you a path to Hades himself."

"We are ready," I say.

"Here, son. When you are ready to come back, break this pendant, and it will open the portal again."

"Thank you, Father."

A portal opens before us just wide enough for Olive and me to pass through. I hold Olive's hand, and we walk through.

We walk up to the massive doors of Hades's throne room. They groan as I push them open and we step inside. The air here is hot and thick. The shadows curl at Olive's feet, welcoming her. They seem to be recoiling away from me. I give a breathy chuckle.

"What is it?"

"It seems not only my shadows like to be wrapped around your ankles."

"OMG, Malsumis!" She playfully slaps my arm, then thoughtfully says, "Later."

I grin as we continue to walk to Hades.

He is sitting on his throne when we walk into his main room. A curious glimmer lights up his eyes. He looks us over for a moment.

"Your footsteps echo through my realm. I assume this is not a social visit," he says at last with a cold kindness that only he could convey.

"Her...our bonded is here. We want him back," the words come out sharper than I mean for them to. Olive rests her hand on my arm.

"Mark is here. We sensed him for a moment, but since then, there has been nothing. Can you help us find him?" She asks calmly.

Hade's gaze softens at that.

"I know of whom you speak. I released him," he says plainly. "I do not know his location now."

"You are the king of this realm," I bristle.

"Tartarus is not completely my realm. Most of it is a wound beneath my realm. It has a life of its own," he replies gently.

The silence that follows is enough to bend the air.

"Is he...gone?" Olive's voice trembles, and I pull her close.

Hades rises from his throne, not in intimidation but more out of respect. He stops a few feet away from us.

"I cannot tell you where he is. I *can* tell you he is at peace," he says.

Olive blinks, her lips parting, not knowing whether to cry or hope.

"What does that mean? Is he dead? Trapped? Free?" I question.

"It means wherever he is, his suffering has stopped. His spirit is quiet. His fear has lifted."

Olive's hand goes to her heart as if she is trying to get some kind of feeling from Mark.

"Is he alive?" I continue to press.

"Life and death are not the boundaries that define him anymore. Whatever path he walks, he walks it without torment. If you seek him, continue, but know that he is not lost. Only…hidden. Perhaps, he is becoming something new." Hades says thoughtfully.

"We will find him," I vow.

"I expect nothing less," Hades says, stepping back to his throne. "After all, souls rarely sever their ties to gods who love them this fiercely."

Olive and I take our leave and walk out of Hades's throne room. As we walk down the dimly lit hall, neither of us speaks for several moments. The air between us feels heavy with unspoken sadness.

"What do we do now?" Olive stops and asks.

"We go back and find a way to rip apart the heavens to find him."

"There has to be a less violent way."

"We will try your way first," I smile at her.

I take the pendant from my pocket and break it.

When we walk through the portal to Father's realm, it is completely dark outside except for a campfire in front of his house. We see Father, Anastasia, Gluskap, and Set all waiting for us. Set makes it to us first.

"Where is he?"

"We don't know. All we know is he isn't in Tartarus, and he is at peace." Olive informs him. The disappointment on his face is heartbreaking. He misses his friend. I didn't realize what an impact Mark had on those around him. I knew he was a good male, but I should have given him more of a chance. I should have recognized the signs of him being Olive's mortal mate.

"Malsumis, are you okay?" Father asks.

"Yes. No. I do not know how to explain."

"Come, let us speak alone."

"It's okay, I will go by the fire with the others. I love you," Olive says.

"I love you, my Olive," I lean down and kiss her before she goes off with the others.

"What is it you are feeling, Malsumis?"

"I do not know really. I did not know Mark well, but I have this emptiness now that he is gone. I practically hated him when I was trapped, but now I wish he were here. How does this make sense?"

"Some of it is the bond. Because he was or is Olive's mate, that means he and you are bonded. That much you know. This situation is rare but not unheard of in our world. Now your bond is whatever you want from it. A kinship, friendship, a companionship. That is why you feel so connected to him. At the very least, I feel like you two would be friends."

"It feels very odd having this conversation with you, but thank you, Father. I understand."

"Son, I am here for you. I am sorry I have not always been."

"I am glad you are now."

Father pulls me in for a hug, and when he releases me, there are tears in his eyes.

"Come on, Set was talking about something called a s'more, and I really want to try one before he eats them all." Father jokes.

Olive and I go home, and it has been a few mortal days. We all tried calling out for Mark with no answer or any sense of him at all. We discussed with Father the possibility of finding a way into the heavens to find him. He said he had never done such, but he would speak with Ra and try to reach Zeus. To say that we are feeling defeated would be an understatement.

Olive stops in the living room and turns to me with her arms wrapped around herself.

"I wanted him to be alive."

"I did too," I whispered as I paused beside her.

"He is at peace through. He isn't suffering in Tartarus. That is good. Right?"

"It is. We tried, my Love. He knew we were searching for him. He felt us too."

She leaned into me, and I wrapped her in my arms, pulling her close.

"It hurts, though. I didn't expect it to hurt. I barely knew him."

"Being bonded to him changed the way you look at things."

"It did," I admit.

There is a long silence between us, just holding each other. Olive looks up at me.

"I am glad he is at peace. I know we will continue to search, but even if he stays far from us, just knowing he is at peace helps."

"It does help. Peace is better than the pain and suffering he was in. If he is resting, then that is something beautiful."

Chapter 56: Olive

We haven't given up hope of ever finding Mark, but we are happy to know that he is no longer in Tartarus, suffering. We couldn't save him, but knowing he was saved from that fate gives us some sort of peace as well.

Malsumis and I decided to have a quiet evening at home. Set of course thought that should include him, and we didn't have the heart to tell him no. He has felt the loss of Mark, too. They had become fast friends, and I know everything weighs heavily on Set, too.

Our quiet night at home has turned into a deafening one with these two. I admittedly messed up letting them pick an action movie to watch. The moment the hero sprints across the screen with a flaming sword, Malsumis shouts out.

"THIS IS MY KIND OF CINEMA! FIRE! BAD DECISIONS! UNNECESSARY BACKFLIPS!"

"Please. I could out backflip that mortal with my eyes closed and one hand tied behind my back," Set says confidently.

"Oh yeah? I bet you would eat asphalt before you could stick the landing," Malsumis spins toward him.

"I am the embodiment of storms and desert fury! I have never once eaten asphalt, thank you."

I am still snuggled up to Malsumis when I start laughing at them.

"Oh, you think we are funny?" Malsumis asks as he begins to tickle my side. I laugh so hard I snort. They both stop and look at me.

"You snorted!" Set says laughing.

"That has to be the sweetest sound I have ever heard," Malsumis adds.

"Oh shut up and watch your movie!" I laugh.

On screen, the hero leaps from a burning building.

"YES! Show them that you have no regard for your skeleton!" Set yells.

"Pointless dramatic roll! Do it again, but angrier!" Malsumis calls to the hero.

"He can't hear you two, but everyone else in the neighborhood can," I laugh.

Just then, there is a knock at the door.

"See, someone probably called the cops!" I teased.

"I will get it," Set jumps up and heads for the door.

"It is not even your house," Malsumis jokes.

"You wound me, Mal," Set gasps.

Set opens the door and staggers back in shock.

Malsumis and I jump from the couch.

Then we hear a familiar voice.

"Can I come in?"

Set rushes back to the door, laughing.

Malsumis runs over.

I stand frozen.

Malsumis turns and looks at me, eyes wide.

Still, I don't move.

This isn't real.

He steps into the room.

I can't breathe.

Mark is standing in my living room.

Not a ghost.

Not a memory.

Not a dream.

Alive.

Different but Alive.

I pressed my trembling hand over my mouth. Tears fall before I realize I'm crying.

"I hope I'm not intruding," Mark says, smiling softly at me.

"You were dead." Malsumis walks up beside him.

"I was. The Fates disagreed with that decision."

Malsumis extended his hand for Mark to take.

"I am glad you're back. We tried to break into Tartarus, but by the time we did, you were gone." Malsumis tells him. Mark takes his hand and pulls him into a hug.

"I know I felt you both. Thank you. I not only chose her. I chose you, too."

Malsumis nods his head in acknowledgement.

Mark walks over to where I am still frozen in place. I look at Malsumis. Not asking permission, but if this is real. He nods, and I look back at Mark, who is right in front of me.

"What, I fight my way through Tartarus to get back to my girl, and I can't get a Hi?" Mark teases. I give him a look. "There she is."

"Set and I are going to give you two some time alone. Not forever, Mark, she is mine too," Malsumis teases. TEASES! WITH MARK! I think I'm going to pass out.

Malsumis kisses my head and is gone.

"Hi," I whisper.

"Hi, baby."

I reach out with shaky fingers, afraid he is going to vanish like a mirage.

I touch warm skin.

A sob burst from me.

I throw my arms around him. He catches me instantly, holding on as he will never let go. I hope he doesn't.

"I thought I lost you forever."

"Never, my girl. I will always find my way back to you."

"We tried to get to you. We tried…" I start crying again.

"I know, I could feel you. You kept me going. Kept me fighting."

He takes my face in his hands, and we stand there just looking at each other for several moments. Neither quite believes this moment is real. His eyes are still that bright, beautiful green, but now there are subtle flecks of gold.

He leans in slowly, almost like he is unsure if I am ready to kiss him. I am more than ready. I close the distance between us. As soon as our lips meet, it is like a flame is ignited. My hands tangle in the back of his hair. When I bite down on his bottom lip, he growls a moan, and then our clothes are gone.

"Really?"

"I have spent too long not looking at you, not touching you, not inside you," he says in a low tone, and then he is back on me.

His lips crash back onto mine. His hands move over my body, memorizing every curve again. I match his eagerness. He stops kissing me, and I feel him step away. When I open my eyes, we are no longer in the living room. We are in our room. For several moments, we just look at each other, almost like neither of us can believe this is real. He is different. He is the same. He is *something* different.

"What are you?"

"Yours," he answers before he kneels in front of me. "You are the only one I will ever kneel to my Goddess. Now, lie on the bed and spread your legs." This is my Mark.

I obey.

He is on me as soon as I am in position. He starts pressing hot kisses across my collarbone, working his way to my breast. As he takes a nipple into his mouth, he pushes his fingers into me.

"You are so wet for me, pretty girl," he says in a gravelly voice.

He curls his fingers and hits the spot that drives me wild just as he nips at one of my nipples. I moan as I arch my back in pleasure. He continues to hit that spot over and over as he trails down my stomach with his tongue. I let out a breathy moan.

"Do not come until I tell you to." I whimper, and he gives a low chuckle.

He begins sucking on my clit.

"Mark!"

"Do. Not. Come," he commands.

He pulls his fingers from me. He licks me from bottom to top in one lazy, broad stroke on his tongue.

I begin to see stars.

"Olive," he growls.

"Mark! I can't…"

Despite his protest, he pushes his fingers inside of me and flicks my clit with his tongue, helping me ride out my orgasm.

"You have been a bad girl, baby."

"What. Are you. Going. To do?" I breathe.

"Fuck you however I want."

I would let him do that anyway, but hearing him say it has me ready for him again.

"On the floor, on your knees."

I do as he says, knowing what's coming.

He sits at the edge of the bed, then pulls me in by my hair. Not enough to hurt, just enough to be sexy. This man.

I give him a long, lazy lick as he did for me, and his grip on my hair tightens slightly. I take him in my mouth and stroke him as I suck.

"Fuck baby."

He leans back on one arm, keeping one hand in my hair, and begins to thrust into my mouth.

"You are taking me so well."

He leans his head back and moans.

"I am going to fucking come if you keep doing this. Stand up." I do as he says.

He clears off the drawers closest to him and sets me on them.

"Perfect. Slide to the edge."

I get to the edge, and he is in me.

"It has been too long, baby. You feel so good around me," he says as he thrusts into me.

I wrap my legs around him, urging him further inside. He leans in and kisses me with a fire and passion that only he has. He breaks the kiss to move to my shoulder.

"Mark. I…can't…"

"Come, baby."

I begin my spiral, clenching around him. He slows his pace, taking in my pleasure around him. He begins to quicken his pace again and chase his own release. He bites down on my shoulder as he comes. There is an intense heat from his bite, a heat I have never felt before. I don't give it much thought as I listen to his moans as he comes.

We stay still for a bit, just being close.

"Come on, my girl, let's get a shower," he says with a smirk.

Chapter 57: Mark

Even after a night with my girl, I still can't believe I am back with her. It feels like a cruel joke that Tartarus is playing on me.

As I lie here holding her, I am afraid to close my eyes, because when I do, I see Tartarus. I see the spirit of the girl in the river, I feel all the sadness and anger, the defeat, and fear.

"Mark," she says sleepily.

"Yes, baby," I say, kissing her head.

"What's wrong?"

"Nothing."

"Don't lie to me. Something is bothering you."

"It's just…I'm afraid this isn't real, that this is another game. Another trick Tartarus is playing."

"Oh. I'm not going to pretend to know what you have been through, but I assure you this is real. What can I do to help you?"

"I don't know really. I guess it will take some time."

"We are here for you."

"We?"

"Me, of course. Malsumis, Set, Gluskap, and Tala"

"Tala?"

"Malsumis and Kap's dad."

"Kap?"

"It is what we call Gluskap now," she giggles. " I guess I need to catch you up on a few things."

"Probably," I laugh.

"We should probably let Malsumis come home. He has been asking for an hour now," she laughs. "He is not very patient."

"Is that what that feeling has been? It is like a nagging feeling in the back of my head."

"Yep, you will get used to it and learn how to listen to it. It's difficult at first."

She slides on an oversized t-shirt, and she gives me a pair of grey sweat pants, and we climb back in bed. The next thing I know, Malsumis is coming through the bedroom door and climbing into the bed on the other side of Olive.

He isn't jealous.

He isn't angry.

He just missed her.

"It has been too long, my Olive," he says, in between peppering her with kisses.

"It has been one night, my love."

"One night too long. Thank you for taking care of our girl, Mark, but from now on, you both are stuck with me."

"You are so dramatic," Olive giggles as he continues to kiss her neck.

I don't know what I expected, but this is not it. It is way better, but definitely not what I thought would be happening right now. I know there is some sort of bond there with Mal and me, but he has accepted it and is actually trying. I am so happy in this moment. Is this real?

"It's real, babe," Olive leans over and whispers in my ear. I lean in and kiss her.

"No. My turn," Mal growls, pulls Olive on top of him, and frees himself from his pants. Fuck, that is hot. Is this fucking happening right now?

He begins to guide her rhythm, and she reaches over for me. I go over and kiss her, still not believing this is real.

"HOLY FUCK! YES I AM IN!" Set exclaims as he walks in the door, taking his shirt off. I must admit he is sexy as hell, but he isn't getting anywhere near what is mine.

"NO!" Mal and I yell at the same time.

"Come on, that is all you guys ever say," Set grumbles as he walks back out the door and down the stairs. Well, so much for the hottest morning of my existence.

The bedroom door slams shut.

"Where were we?" Mal asks, beginning to have Olive move again.

"What about Set?" I ask.

"You can go be with him or stay with us. You choose." Mal says in a deep, low voice.

"Fuck, I'm not leaving this."

I slide Olive's shirt off, baring her to us.

She continues her rhythm on top of Mal as I move behind her and pull her hair enough that she leans her head to the side. I begin sucking and licking her neck, earning me her breathy moans that drive me crazy. Apparently, they have the same effect on Mal because he starts to thrust into her as she continues to move. I grab her hips and help her in her movements, and am rewarded with moans from both of them.

"Malsumis…Mark…" Olive breathes. Malsumis reaches forward and begins to circle her clit until she screams out in pleasure.

"Fuck…yes…Olive," Mal moans before he comes.

As they both come down, I continue to kiss Olive's neck.

"You did so well, pretty girl," I tell her.

"Where do you want me?" she asks me.

"This was for Mal, not me."

"If our girl wants more, who are we to deny her?" Mal responds.

"Fuck. Get on your hands and knees, goddess."

She visibly shivers, and her nipples harden in excitement. Mal just smirks.

I push into her from behind and grab her hair and pull back. Mal positions himself in front of her so he can talk her through everything. I slap her perfect ass, and she sucks in a breath.

"You're doing so well, my Olive." Mal praises.

"That's my girl, you can take this, can't you?" I add.

We are answered with her moans, and I know she is getting close to coming again.

"Are you going to come again, baby?"

"Yes," she breathes.

"Mal, help our girl."

He slides down, takes one of her nipples in his mouth, and begins to rub circles around her already sensitive clit.

"Oh, I'm coming!"

As she comes around me, I lose control and am coming soon myself. We all lie in the bed. Mal is on one side of Olive, and I am on the other.

"Real?" I whisper to Olive.

"Definitely real, babe."

After we all take a shower, we head down to a waiting Set, who I honestly had forgotten was here.

"Why do you guys always lock me out? I am excellent in the boudoir. Mal can attest to that." Set protests.

I turn to look, surprised at Mal.

"Shut up, Set," is all Mal says and winks at me. Okay. I know this can't be real life. Mal has never been friendly to me, and would definitely never have shared Olive with me. If this is a dream, though, I don't want to wake up.

"We are sorry we made you wait, Set. What is it that you needed?" Olive asks.

"Well, I thought that since Mark is back, we should have a small gathering. With food and friends."

"Mark just got back. I don't know if he feels ready for that yet."

"I think I would be okay with that. We can plan for a few days from now, and that will give me time to catch up on excuses for why I have been gone and get settled back in my house."

"At your house?" Olive asks.

"Do I still have a house?"

"Yes, you do. I just… never mind, you're right. That sounds perfect. I will let the girls know. I will be right back."

Olive leaves the room and immediately feels like I have done something wrong.

"Oh, you are in trouble!" Set teases.

"Okay, what did I do?"

"Mates do not live apart," Mal answers.

"Fuck. I don't want to be away from her. I just didn't want to assume that I lived here now. What do I do now?"

"You fix it," Mal says.

"Thanks, that helps so much, Mal."

"Go to her and explain, you idiot," Set laughs. "But hurry, you owe me a game on that little box of yours. I have gotten good!"

I walk into Olive's library, which used to be the primary bedroom, and find her in a chair with her back to me. I watch her for a second and see her shoulders shake slightly. She is crying because of me. I am such an idiot.

I walk around her and kneel before her. She looks up at me and smiles weakly.

"Oh, sorry. I got distracted. I will call Jennifer and Candy now."

"Olive. I am sorry. I didn't know that you wanted me here. This is yours and Mal's place. I didn't want to assume that I had a place here."

"Of course, you have a place here. You are my mate, Mal's bonded! What did you think was going to happen? That I could just let you go again? I just got you back, I can't be without you again!" She is getting upset and starting to panic. Mal pokes his head in to make sure everything is okay. I love how protective he is of our girl. I give him a nod and refocus on Olive.

"Baby, it's okay. Breathe for me, you are never losing me again," I comfort her as I take her into my arms.

"I'm sorry. I am being selfish. You need to do what is right for you. I just panicked. Of course, you should be comfortable. I mean, it's not like I even have to drive to you now." She says.

"No, baby, I am not leaving you. You and Mal are stuck with me. I am getting my things and moving in, so you better make some room in the closet."

"You don't have to just because I freaked out."

"I'm moving in because I love you. I want to be with you. Wake up with you, go to bed with you. Of course, fuck you whenever I want."

That earns me a slap on the arm and a dirty look. There's my girl.

"Now let's invite Jenny and Candy, then I have some catching up to do."

Chapter 58: Malsumis

Set staggers back, and I think the worst, so I jump up ready to fight, but then I see who is at the door. It is Mark. It seems impossible, but this is Mark. He is something different, but he is still Mark. I can feel it.

I look over to Olive. She is frozen in place. I give her some space to realize that this is real while I greet Mark. He seems a little surprised that I am happy to see him. He does not realize how much I have changed and how much I have accepted our situation. I tell him that we never stopped looking for him, and I am shocked when he pulls me into a hug, but it feels right, like hugging an old companion.

"I know I felt you both. Thank you. I not only chose her. I chose you, too."

Even after everything, he thinks I am worthy of being chosen, too. He does not know how much weight those words hold with me.

He walks over to a still shocked Olive. She looks to me as if she needs confirmation that this is real. I give her a nod.

"We should give them some time alone," Set suggests.

"I think that is a good idea."

I walk over.

"Set and I are going to give you two some time alone. Not forever, Mark, she is mine too," I joke as I slap him on the back.

We laugh, and then I kiss my Olive. Set and I then head to Mark's old house, where Set has been staying sometimes, to give Olive and Mark some time to catch up.

I told myself that giving them one night was reasonable. I have survived eons without them. This should be nothing. I instantly regret my decision to leave. It feels wrong.

"I'm doing it. I am staying away," I say as I sink into the couch beside Set.

"You said that five minutes ago. Congratulations, you are still here," Set says sarcastically.

"Shit, something may be wrong. I need to go back."

"What? Why?"

"I can feel their emotions. They are heightened. What if something is wrong?"

"Uh, I think something is right," Set laughs.

"Fuck." I know he is right. I can *feel* both of their heightened emotional states.

"You can feel *that*?"

"Yes, and it is torture," I say, adjusting on the couch.

"Try not to sense them," he says, handing me a beer.

"Thanks for the great advice. You know, I think it is working."

"Ass."

"Sorry. This isn't easy, being away from them, especially Olive. It is a weakness I need to work on."

 "It is not a weakness, Mal." "It feels like it," I snort.

"It is an attachment. It is love. It is something that not everyone gets to experience."

"I am sorry."

"Let's play a game. I have been practicing, but I need more to beat Mark." Set suggests.

"Sure, why not?" I give in.

Set gives me a controller.

"It is simple. You move. You attack. You DO NOT alter reality."

"Why do they give you so many buttons if you do not use them all at once?" I ask.

"Just press A to start."

I pressed every button. My character spun, jumped, crouched, and immediately fell off a cliff.

"I have killed him," I say, looking at Set.

"You walked him forward into the void," Set says, pinching the bridge of his nose.

We restart the game.

"Okay. Left stick moves. Right stick turns. Triggers are…"

My character starts vibrating violently.

"Why is he vibrating?" Set freezes.

The screen flickers, the character multiplies, and starts dancing.

"I improved him."

"You are not allowed to influence the code, Mal!"

"No powers. Swear it."

"Fine. Fine. Mostly no powers."

We continue playing until the dawn started to break outside the window.

I call for Olive and Mark.

"I made it the night," I say.

I call again.

"That you did. I am proud of you." I call

again.

"I am going to make us some breakfast. Eggs and bacon?"

"Sure, that sounds great." Knowing fully well that I will be gone as soon as Olive or Mark answers me.

I call again.

Set brings breakfast in, and we begin to eat.

I call again.

Olive answers.

"We should…"

I do not hear what Set says next because I have already gone back to them.

Chapter 59: Olive

It has been a week since Mark came back. Honestly, it has been like a dream. Everything is falling into place. We are all growing closer. He and Set are besties.

Today is our little party for Mark's homecoming. Set, and I am getting everything ready to cook later while Mark takes Malsumis out to teach him how to drive. I cannot wait to hear how that goes!

I am balancing a tray of veggie skewers in one hand while I carry a tray of steaks in the other. Set is hanging string lights around the deck. We have a fire pit area set up in the yard. Anyone looking in would never know we are a house full of immortals and gods.

"Why do we have to do everything by hand? I could have this all hung by now," Set complains.

"What if one of the neighbors saw the lights hanging themselves? How would I explain that?" I ask, setting down the trays of food.

"I guess," he says, finishing up. "So, just a simple homecoming gathering?"

"Yes. Mortal and simple."

"That is it?" Set arches a brow. "No fanfare? No thunder? No choirs calling out, "Behold, the lost one returns"? I mean, as far as we know, he is the first of his kind. He deserves something more." "Mark would hate all of that," I huff, a quiet laugh.

"You're right," Set concedes.

"He wants normal. A yard, food that might burn, friends who complain about mosquitoes," I pause, gathering myself. "He dreamt about this. Even when he didn't think he would ever come back."

"Does he remember everything from Tartarus?" Set asks quietly.

"Yes. The pain, the fear, all of it," I meet Set's eyes. "The love stayed too, though." Set nods, looking sincere.

"Welcome home, sorry about the eternal trauma," he says.

"Thank you for being here," I say with a hint of a laugh.

"There is nowhere I would rather be," then he smirks. "Well, maybe in your bed."

"I can hear you, desert menace," Malsumis says as he walks up and wraps his arms around me from behind.

Mark comes to view in front of me with one of his achingly beautiful smiles that makes my breath catch.

"Hi, baby."

"Hi," I answer with a smile of my own. Mark leans in and kisses me.

"See, this is hot!" Set exclaims.

"Set," Mark and Malsumis say at the same time.

"Fine, fine."

"So how did the lesson go?" I ask, changing the subject.

"Well, it was educational," Malsumis says, coming around to sit at the table.

"Malsumis, what happened?" I ask.

"I did not destroy the car," he answers.

"That is not as reassuring as you think it is," I raise my brows and look to Mark, who is now sitting between Set and Malsumis.

"He says the car is temperamental and hates him." That gets Mark an elbow in the side from Mal.

"It does hate me. I was doing everything you said, and it still misbehaved!"

"You almost hit somebody. Several somebodies!" Mark laughs.

"I wish I had been there!" Set laughs.

"You would have loved it when Mark screamed a pitch that only dogs can hear and then said his soul left his body." Now we are all laughing.

"He kept waving at people!"

"They were honking at me!"

"Because you almost ran into them!"

We are laughing when Jennifer and Candy walk through the back gate.

"You started the party without us?" Jennifer called out.

"Of course not! Come on up, we are still waiting for Kap and Tala." I tell her.

Before they make it up the stairs to the deck, I turn to the boys.

"No powers, no auras, no prophetic statements. Remember, we are mortal."

"I am the picture of mortal subtlety," Set says.

"You set the toaster on fire last week," Malsumis snorts as he walks to the grill to light it. A fire begins immediately.

"Malsumis!" I whisper yell at him.

"They are not up here yet," he shrugs. I roll my eyes at him, and Mark is at my side before I know it.

"Roll those eyes again, pretty girl. We will take care of that attitude later," he says into my ear, sending shivers throughout my body.

"Oh, come on. I can hear you!" Set throws his hands up in exasperation.

"We brought dessert!" Candy exclaims as she walks up.

Jennifer and Candy walk over to where Mark and I are standing, and both hug him.

"I am surprised that you are throwing this party, Olive," Jennifer says to me while Candy and Mark are chatting. "What do you mean?"

"Well, after the breakup and now that you have Mal, it has to be weird to have Mark around."

Right on cue, Mark runs his hand down my back and pulls me closer to him. Jennifer and Candy both look confused, but say nothing as Mark continues talking about "his work".

Gluskap, Tala, and Anastasia come out from the house onto the deck. They come over, greet Mark and me, and then go over to Set and Malsumis.

Jennifer and Candy began to fill me in on what I have been missing at the museum. Malsumis announces that it is time to eat, so we all gather around the table and the conversations bubble comfortably about jobs, bad bosses, and terrible dating stories. No one slipping once into an *I once watched civilizations rise and fall* territory.

We head down to the fire pit once we are all finished eating and listen to Tala tell stories about when the world was created. Of course, Jennifer and Candy think they are myths and legends, but the rest of us know better.

I am sitting between Malsumis and Mark with my head on Mal's and Mark's hand on my thigh. I can feel eyes on me from across the fire. Jennifer and Candy are giving me questioning looks. I give them a "I will fill you in later" look. Jennifer looked very unsatisfied with that answer.

Once it starts getting late, we clean up, and Jennifer and Candy corner me in the kitchen.

"Okay, spill it! What is going on?" Jennifer presses.

"Yeah, surely Mal is not okay with Mark touching you like he is," Candy adds.

"Okay, okay! Don't freak out. I am with both of them," I say quickly.

"WHAT!" they both yell.

"Yell louder, please. I don't think the neighbor across the street heard you!"

"Sorry, but what the actual fuck, Olive!" Jennifer says, still in shock. Poor Candy is speechless.

"I said, don't freak out!"

"Are you with them at like the same time?" Jennifer asks.

"Jennifer!" Candy chastises.

"Yes, she is," Mark says from behind me.

"She quite likes it too," Malsumis adds.

"Really, you two. We were having girl talk in here!" I say, arching a brow at them.

"Sorry, baby, continue your girl talk. Don't leave us waiting too long, though," Mark says with a wink and kisses me. Malsumis walks up and pulls me in for a hard kiss, and turns and walks out with Mark.

"That is fucking hot," Jennifer breathes.

"I am going to have to agree," Candy says quietly.

"Well, I don't mean to be a bad hostess, but I have something I need to do."

"More like two somethings!" Jennifer says, and we all break out in the giggles.

Chapter 60: Olive

It has been a month since Mark came home, and we are thriving all together. Currently, I am lying on the couch in Malsumis's arms, both of us reading. Mark and Set are in a battle on their video games on the other side of the room. Everything is perfect. I never thought that my life would be like this.

Once everything felt hollow and lonely, then Malsumis and Mark came into my life and rearranged everything for me. They are filling it with warmth, love, laughter, and devotion. Things I thought I would never have.

I smile at the thought of Malsumis and how he learned to be gentle without losing his fire. Loving him has not been easy. It has been loud, complicated, painful, but honest, real. He discovered love did not weaken him. It made him stronger. It anchors him.

Then there is Mark.

My chest aches softly at his name, a familiar, cherished ache. When we became friends, he confided in me that he was gay. I kept that to myself at his request, but somewhere in our friendship, something shifted for us. I fell for him even though

I thought he was unavailable, and he realized that for him, love was about the person, not their gender. Death separated us twice, but each time we found our way back to one another.

We all have changed.

We are stronger. Softer. Bound by destiny but together by choice.

I close my eyes, letting that truth settle in.

"I love you, my Olive," Malsumis whispers into my ear.

Mark looks over and smiles at us.

For the first time in my existence, the future doesn't feel like something I have to endure. It feels like something I get to share, and I get to share it with them.

<u>EPILOUGE</u>: Malsumis

Six Months Later

I feel it first.

A thread is being gently knotted where there had been none before. I pause mid step in the kitchen, my power curling inward in caution of what I am feeling.

Something new has anchored itself to Olive.

Mark is making his coffee and stops short.

"Hey Mal, I feel something…new with Olive."

"I feel that too."

We meet each other's gaze.

"It's like it isn't just her anymore," he says, unconsciously rubbing his sternum.

"There is a second heartbeat," I say, not quite believing what I am saying. I had dreamt of this, but never thought it would ever actually happen for me. Since I met Olive, I let myself dream again.

Mark's breath hitches, and a nervous laugh escapes, disbelieving and warm all at once.

We both head to the library, where Olive is in her chair, reading.

"Why are you both looking at me like that?" Olive questions.

I kneel before her and gently press my palm over her abdomen. Mark sits beside her and places his hand over mine without hesitation, so we are all joined in this moment.

"There is a beginning inside of you," I say, trying to fight back tears.

"And we're already in love," Mark says, smiling through wet eyes.

Olive freezes.

She laughs, breathless and bright, and pulls us both closer as the truth settles in.

Three hearts listening.

Four hearts beating.

<u>Bonus Scene</u>: Mark

Mal sits in the driver's seat as if the car had personally offended him.

"I do not understand," he says, staring at the steering wheel. "I have watched the rise and fall of civilizations and yet this…beast is beyond my comprehension." He wiggles the wheel aggressively.

"Okay, first rule of our lesson, don't turn the wheel like that, especially while driving. Second, get your foot off the gas." I say as I buckle my seat belt.

"I am not on the gas," Mal replied indignantly.
The engine revs.
"Mal, that pedal is not a footrest."

"Oh," Mal lifts his foot, and the car lurches, then stalls completely.

We sit in silence.

"Did I kill it?"

"You stalled it. The car is fine, though."

"It makes odd noises."

"That is the engine. Now gently turn the key." I instruct.

"I know how to start a car." He turns the key too gently, and nothing happens.

"Do you though?" I tease. "A little more power this time."

He turns it harder, and the engine roars to life.

"I didn't mean use your power!" I say, jumping in surprise.

"Oh, sorry."

We ease out of the parking lot at an approximate speed of a glacier.

A pedestrian passes us. Walking. Faster than us.

"Uh, you can go a little faster."

Mal nods, and the car shoots forward.

"BRAKE!" I scream in a very undignified way.

He slams on the brakes, and the car stops so abruptly that my soul leaves my body for the second time in my life.

"You are very loud," Mal says.

"You almost sent us into the astral plane, so yeah, I was a little concerned. New rule. Pretend the gas pedal is sleeping and you do not want to wake it."

We continue with jerky turns and missing signals. Mal waves at the other drivers honking at him.

"Why are they shouting?"

"They're mad."

"At me?"

"Yes."

"Do they want the plague? Because I can arrange that."

"NO MAL!"

He just laughs.

When we finally pull back into the parking lot, the car is somehow still intact.

"I'm alive!" I exclaim, slumping into my seat.

"You are dramatic. I also learn a lot. The car is fragile. The horn is rude. You scream like a female." Mal smiles.

“You are never driving my car again. Lessons over.” I tease.

Mal slaps my leg and laughs.

“I need a drink,” I groan.

Glossary Of Gods

<u>Malsumis</u>- trickster, chaos god in Abenaki mythology

<u>Gluskap/Glooskap</u>- a god who helps humans in Abenaki mythology

<u>Great Spirit</u>- a supreme being, governing over life in Native American cultures. In this story, he is Tala.

<u>Set</u>- God of deserts, storms, and violence in Egyptian mythology

<u>Ra</u>- God of the sun, King of the Gods in Egyptian mythology

<u>Anubis</u>- God of mummification, God of the Afterlife in Egyptian Mythology

<u>Hathor</u>- Goddess of love, joy, and beauty, also helped usher souls into the afterlife in Egyptian mythology.

<u>Thoth</u>- God of wisdom, writing, and magic in Egyptian mythology

<u>Eris</u>- Goddess of discord and strife in Greek mythology

<u>Zeus</u>- King of the Gods in Greek Mythology

<u>Hades</u>- God of the underworld in Greek mythology

The Fates- three sisters who control the fate of all life. Clotho spins the thread at birth, Lachesis measures the length, and Atropos cuts it at death.

Hera- Queen of the Olympian Gods, Zeus's wife